Fuddy Meers

Fuddy Meers

David Lindsay-Abaire

THE OVERLOOK PRESS
WOODSTOCK & NEW YORK

First published in the United States in 2001 by
The Overlook Press, Peter Mayer Publishers, Inc.
Lewis Hollow Road
Woodstock, New York 12498
www.overlookpress.com

Copyright © 1999 by David Lindsay-Abaire

Library of Congress Cataloging-in-Publication Data

Lindsay-Abaire, David.
Fuddy Meers / David Lindsay-Abaire
p. cm.
to come

Book design and type formatting by Bernard Schleifer
Manufactured in the United States of America
FIRST EDITION
1 3 5 7 9 8 6 4 2
ISBN 1-58567-122-3 (pbk)
ISBN 0-7394-1473-9 (hc)

Introduction

"Your memory is a monster; you forget—it doesn't. It simply files things away. It keeps things from you —and summons them to your recall with a will all its own You think you have a memory, but it has you."
—JOHN IRVING, *A Prayer for Owen Meany*

I hate introductions. Mostly because I'm not very good at introducing myself. Or at introducing my work. Here's a little scene illustrating a typical introduction for me:

> DAVID LINDSAY-ABAIRE
> Hello. I guess this is my table. My name is David

> MARGIE
> I'm Margie. I'm the groom's aunt. Who do *you* know?

> DAVID LINDSAY-ABAIRE
> The bride. We were in college together.

> MARGIE
> Oh. Nice.
> *(long, comfortable pause)*

> MARGIE
> So what do you do, David?

> DAVID LINDSAY-ABAIRE
> I'm a playwright.

MARGIE

Oh yeah? Have you seen "Cats"? Bob and I saw it last spring. I
bet they get very hot in those furry costumes. Have you seen it?

DAVID LINDSAY-ABAIRE

No, I haven't.

MARGIE

It's very good. Bob didn't care for it, but I thought it was very
good. Are your plays like "Cats"?

DAVID LINDSAY-ABAIRE

Not really, no.

MARGIE

Oh that's too bad. I really liked "Cats." Especially Rum Tum
Tugger. He was *very* good. Do you know the actor who played
Rum Tum Tugger?

DAVID LINDSAY-ABAIRE

No I don't

MARGIE

I wish *he* was at my table.
    (*an afterthought*)
No offense.

DAVID LINDSAY-ABAIRE

None taken. I had the same thought.

    (*Another uncomfortable pause. Margie wonders if
    she's just been insulted.*)

MARGIE

Do you write comedy or drama?

DAVID LINDSAY-ABAIRE

That's a hard question.

MARGIE

It is? Why? Why is that a hard question?

DAVID LINDSAY-ABAIRE
Well, it's such a subjective—

MARGIE
(interrupting)
Is what you write funny?

DAVID LINDSAY-ABAIRE
Mostly.

MARGIE
Then that's a comedy. When something is funny, we call it a
comedy. Really, as a playwright, you should know that.
(calls off)
Bob. this playwright doesn't know what comedy means!
(back to David)
Bob can't hear me. He's at the bar. Bob drinks too much. So
do I. I'm drunk right now. Are you?

DAVID LINDSAY-ABAIRE
No.

MARGIE
Really? I thought everyone gets drunk at weddings. You're not
gonna put me in a play, are you? If you do, I'll sue you!
(laughs uproariously)
I'm kidding. You can put me in a play if you want, just make
sure Susan Lucci plays me. I *love* Susan Lucci. Did you see
"Annie Get Your Gun"?

DAVID LINDSAY-ABAIRE
I didn't.

MARGIE
Oh, she was very good. Bob didn't care for her, but I think she
was *very* good.
(downs some Scotch)
So do you have a play I'd know the name of?

DAVID LINDSAY-ABAIRE
Maybe. "Fuddy Meers"?

MARGIE

What's it called?

DAVID LINDSAY-ABAIRE

"Fuddy Meers."

MARGIE

No, I don't know that play. Was it on Broadway?

DAVID LINDSAY-ABAIRE

Off-Broadway.

MARGIE

(sadly)
Awww.

DAVID LINDSAY-ABAIRE

You know, the most exciting new American plays are in fact
being mounted Off-Broadway, not on.

MARGIE

Whatever makes you feel better, sweetheart.
(downs another shot of Scotch)
So what's your play about?

DAVID LINDSAY-ABAIREE

It's about a woman who finds a Henway.

MARGIE

A Henway? What's a Henway?

DAVID LINDSAY-ABAIRE

About six pounds.

MARGIE

(long pause)
Is that a joke?

DAVID LINDSAY-ABAIRE

Sort of.

MARGIE

I hope your play is funnier than that.

DAVID LINDSAY-ABAIRE

I was mostly avoiding the question. It's hard to talk about what a play's about so—

MARGIE

You're kinda cagey, aren't ya?

DAVID LINDSAY-ABAIRE

Am I?

MARGIE
(Margie eyes him suspiciously.)
What's your play called again?

DAVID LINDSAY-ABAIRE

"Fuddy Meers."

MARGIE

Funny-what?

DAVID LINDSAY-ABAIRE

"*Fuddy* . . . Meers."

MARGIE

Fuddy Meyers? What is that, someone's name?

DAVID LINDSAY-ABAIRE

No, it's—

MARGIE

Say it again.

DAVID LINDSAY-ABAIRE

"*Fuddy* . . . *Meers.*"

MARGIE

I still can't understand what you're saying

DAVID LINDSAY-ABAIRE

It's called "Arcadia."

MARGIE

Oh! "Arcadia"! I *love* "Arcadia"!
    (calls off)
Bob, this young nun wrote "Arcadia"! Bob!
    (turns back)
He can't hear me. Doesn't matter, he didn't care for "Arcadia"
anyway. No offense.

So you can understand my fear of introductions.

I'm also a little wary of saying too much about the script because I'm
paranoid about giving anything away. The surprises in "Fuddy Meers" are so
important to the world of the play, and they contribute substantially to the
enjoyment of it. Ideally, I'd like the audience (or in this case the reader) to
approach the world of "Fuddy Meers" the way my main character does: as a
totally game, fun-loving amnesiac with few judgments, and no preconceived
notions of what to expect. "Fuddy Meers" is a ride. Get onboard. Enjoy it.
Have fun. Let it surprise you. Let it scare it you. And if you feel like vomit-
ing when you get off, my apologies. Besides that, I don't want to say too much
about the play.

I *will* say I like my title. I offer that up because in the history of the play
it's been a major topic of discussion. That exchange up above with Margie
wasn't really exaggerated. When someone asks the title of my play, if they
haven't heard of it, I inevitably have to repeat it two or three times, and then
give the explanation of what it means and why it's the title of the play, and at
that point the person who asked about it is glazing over and losing interest,
and I have to jostle them back to consciousness. So I won't explain the title
here. Especially since you have the script in your hands, and you'll find out
soon enough.

But suffice it to say, the title proved a challenge for many. One artistic
director went so far as to say he wouldn't produce the play unless I changed
the title.

I explained why I liked the title. It's literally and thematically connected
to the central image of the story being told. The title is whimsical. It's warped.

It's enigmatic. It's a little scary (some people mishear the title as "Muddy Fears," equally appropriate I suppose). The title is everything I hope the play is.

The artistic director's response was, "That's great if you know the play. But if you don't, then the words "Fuddy Meers" don't tell me anything. It's a confusing title. What does it mean to the guy on the street? Its gibberish. How am I going to get audiences in the door with a title like that?" He of course had very valid points, but then MTC came along and said they'd produce it, title intact, so his ultimatum became a moot point. (He's producing the play next season, by the way. It's still called "Fuddy Meers.")

Let me also give a little background of the play. (This is the customary point in the introduction where it essentially turns into a weepy thank-you note to anyone and everyone I've ever met. If that sort of thing doesn't interest you, I suggest you skip ahead and start reading the play).

"Fuddy Meers" was first written and developed at the Juilliard School's Lila Acheson Wallace American Playwrights Program, under the direction of Marsha Norman and Christopher Durang. I am terribly indebted to my teachers, my classmates, and the actors at Juilliard for everything they contributed to the creation of this play. Thanks also to Jessica Bauman, who directed the wonderful workshop production of "Fuddy Meers" at Juilliard.

In the summer of 1998, I was lucky enough to attend the National Playwrights Conference at the Eugene O'Neill Theatre Centre, where the play was workshopped, and where I received invaluable support and insight from Artistic Director Lloyd Richards, my director William Partlan, my dramaturg Willy Holtzman, as well as the wonderful actors, designers, interns, and everyone else up at that bucolic haven in Waterford, Connecticut.

The Manhattan Theatre Club production opened in New York in October of 1999. It was everything I hoped the play could be and more. The stars aligned, and it seemed every collaborator understood the play and knew where I was coming from (I believe the consensus was Mars). They collectively embraced the strange and wacky world of "Fuddy Meers" in a great big theatrical bear-hug. They understood that the play could be whimsical and silly, and still be very real and painful at its center. They knew to temper the sweetness with a dark edge. The tonal shifts in the play can make for a very tricky line to walk, but my collaborators walked it expertly. From David Petrarca's spotless direction, to Santo Loquasto's ingeniously clever set and costumes. From Brian MacDevitt's eye-popping lights, to Bruce Ellman's pitch-perfect sound design, and Jason Robert Brown's playful and haunting music, I could not have been in better hands.

And that sentiment goes double for my amazing cast of actors. Robert Stanton was riotously unhip as Richard. Keith Knobbs was loathsome and poignant as the quintessential nightmare of a teenager. The deliciously manic Lisa Gorlitsky broke a sweat every night, while the wildly inventive Mark McKinney did double-duty wringing laughs from a foul-mouthed hand-puppet. Patrick Breen managed to straddle both worlds of the play at once, flying between lovable goofball to raging maniac in the blink of a blind eye. And Marylouise Burke, who went on to win a Drama Desk Award for her stunningly articulate performance, managed to be fierce, loving and gut-wrenchingly funny while barely uttering a single word of English.

And what can I possibly say about the radiant J. Smith-Cameron? From our very first rehearsal at the MTC offices to the closing-night performance, she brought a soulful intelligence and heartbreaking humanity to Claire that I could only dream of. She was the sparkling calm at the center of the storm, and she kept the play grounded. funny, and honest. Her talent is Herculean. I am in awe of her brilliance.

When "Fuddy" moved to a commercial run at the Minetta Lane Theatre, Lisa's pregnancy was really starting to show, and Mark McKinney, our resident TV star, had to go on tour with Kids in the Hall. So two new actors stepped in and brought a whole new spin to the play. I am forever grateful for their memorable talents and contributions. John Christopher Jones made Millet an earnest and hilariously sweet misfit. And in Clea Lewis' hands, Heidi became one of the pluckiest, sexiest sirens to ever step into a uniform.

In addition to these folks, I'd like to thank the following people for their contributions and guidance: Letty Aronson, Victoria Bailey, Hilary Bell, Dhana-Marie Branton, Michael Bush, John Buzzetti, David Capparelliotis, Kevin Chamberlin, Matthew Conlon, Jake Cooper, Rebecca Corbett, Christopher Curry, Jean Doumanian, Richard Feldman, Ron Fitzgerald, Erin Gann, Valerie Geffner, Thea Bradshaw Gillies, Avi Glickstein, Jessica Goldberg, Daniel Goldfarb, Robyn Goodman, Barry Grove, Damon Gupton, Ann Hamada, Lisa Harrison, Jeremy Hollingworth, Michael Kahn, Elizabeth Ann Keiser, Joan Kendall, Robert Kerr, T.R. Knight, Fred Koehler, Joe Kraemer, Neal Lerner, Kate Loewald, John Logigian, Leslie Lyles, Quentin Mare, Mary f. McCabe, Lynn Meadow, Jennifer Rae Moore, Mele Nagler, Kristine Neilsen, Christian Parker, Nancy Piccione, Keith Reddin, Randy Reyes, Nancy Ringham, Henny Russell, Edwin Sanchez, Howard Shalwitz, Gay Smith, Rick Sordelet, Helen Stenborg, Alexandra Tolk, David R. White, William Wise, Yvonne Woods, everyone at the Berrilla Kerr Foundation, Primary Stages, Rattlestick Productions, and Dance Theater Workshop.

And most especially my wife, Chris Lindsay-Abaire, whose nurturing insight and sly sense of humor are on every page of this play.

Since my memory is only a little better than Claire's, I apologize if I've left anyone out.

With that, I feel like I'm finished introducing myself and my play. I hope I didn't leave too negative an impression.

Enjoy.

—DAVID LINDSAY-ABAIRE
July, 2000

Fuddy Meers

Fuddy Meers was produced by Manhattan Theatre Club (Lynne Meadow, Artistic Director; Barry Grove, Executive Producer) in New York City on October 12, 1999. It was directed by David Petrarca; the set and costume design were by Santo Loquasto; the lighting design was by Brian Mac Devitt; the sound design was by Bruce Ellman; the original music was by Jason Robert Brown; the fight direction was by Rick Sordelet; and the production stage manager was Thea Bradshaw Gillies. The cast was as follows:

Claire	J. Smith-Cameron
Richard	Robert Stanton
Kenny	Keith Nobbs
Limping Man	Patrick Breen
Gertie	Marylouise Burke
Millet	Mark McKinney
Heidi	Lisa Gorlitsky

Fuddy Meers subsequently transferred to the Minetta Lane Theatre in New York City, produced by Manhattan Theatre Club and Jean Doumanian Productions, on January 27, 2000. It was directed by David Petrarca; the set and costume design were by Santo Loquasto; the lighting design was by Brian MacDevitt; the sound design was by Bruce Ellman; the original music was by Jason Robert Brown; the fight direction was by Rick Sordelet; and the production stage manager was Thea Bradshaw Gillies. The cast was as follows:

Claire	J. Smith-Cameron
Richard	Robert Stanton
Kenny	Keith Nobbs
Limping Man	Patrick Breen
Gertie	Marylouise Burke
Millet	John Christopher Jones
Heidi	Clea Lewis

Design and World of the Play

The audience should experience the play through Claire's eyes as much as possible. With that in mind, the world that the designers create should be a world of incomplete pictures and distorted realities. I imagine the set being representational and fluid. Scenes should flow into focus without interruption. Perhaps as the play moves forward and Claire's vision of her world becomes clearer, so too do her surroundings. For example, each time we revisit Gertie's kitchen, maybe there's a new piece of furniture, or there's a wall where there wasn't one before. But ultimately this is a world of mirrors and memories. I imagine perhaps scrims and projections that can easily transform a space.

At the same time, Claire's world is like a funhouse, where anything can happen. A floor can drop. A room can suddenly be filled with noise. Something terrifying can pop out of the darkness. Giddiness can turn into horror at the turn of a corner. By no means do I want the funhouse imagery literally represented on stage, but maybe a few pieces of furniture are a bit oversized or askew (nothing too stylized or cartoonish). Claire lives in an unsettling world where mad fun and genuine danger are wrapped around each other. The design should help bring this world to life, and include the audience on the ride.

Cast

Claire: about 40—a generally sunny woman with amnesia
Richard: about 40—a chatty, friendly, sometimes nervous, man
Kenny: 17—a troubled teen
Limping Man: about 40—a lisping, limping, half-blind, half-deaf
       man with secrets
Gertie: 60's—a clear-headed lady who's had a stroke and can't
       speak properly
Millet: 30's or 40's—an odd man with a puppet
Heidi: 30's or 40's—a tough woman in uniform

Act One

Scene One

(Alarm clock ringing. Lights up on CLAIRE *in a bed. She tries to open her eyes. She looks at the ringing clock, confused. She takes in the room as if for the first time.*
   RICHARD, *in a robe, enters with a mug of coffee, which he puts on* CLAIRE's *side-table.)*

RICHARD
Good morning, huckleberry! How'd you sleep? You sleep well?!

CLAIRE
I'm not sure.

RICHARD
(shuts alarm off)
I think you did. You snored a lot. You slept soundly.

CLAIRE
That's good.

RICHARD
Sounded soundly. Maybe you had bad dreams though.

(He draws the curtains. Sun pours into the room. CLAIRE *squints at the sunlight.)*

CLAIRE
I don't remember dreaming.

RICHARD
(opens closet and flips through clothes)
No, of course not. But you did. We all do. I dreamt I was a
soccer ball and everyone kept kicking me. Whaddaya suppose
that meant?!

CLAIRE
I don't know.

RICHARD
Oh well.
(holds up dress)
How about this today?

CLAIRE
You mean for me?

RICHARD
You like this dress.

CLAIRE
Oh, it's hideous.

RICHARD
You wear it all the time. You wore it to Jackie's Thanksgiving.
(motions to coffee)
That's your coffee. You can drink it.

CLAIRE
Who's Jackie?

RICHARD
Your cousin.

CLAIRE
Oh.
(takes coffee)
Aren't you having coffee?

RICHARD

I don't drink coffee. I had some juice.

CLAIRE

Oh, juice is nice.

RICHARD

No, you don't like juice, sweetheart.

CLAIRE

I don't?

RICHARD

No.

CLAIRE

I don't think I like that dress.

RICHARD

You do.

CLAIRE

I don't.

RICHARD

You do, darling. You like it very much.

CLAIRE

This is very unsettling.

(KENNY *ducks in. He's 17.*)

KENNY

I don't need a ride. I'm taking the bus.

RICHARD

Did you feed the dog?

KENNY

No.

RICHARD

Don't forget, Kenny. Yesterday you forgot.

KENNY
   (as he exits)
That dog's a fat hunk of shit.

RICHARD

That's Kenny.

CLAIRE

He smells like ribbon candy.

RICHARD

He smokes marijuana.

CLAIRE

That can't be good for him.

RICHARD

I'm hoping it's a phase.
   (picking up puzzle books)
I'm throwing out these search-a-word puzzles. They've been lying around for a couple weeks.

CLAIRE

Oh, I love search-a-word puzzles!
   (beat)
Don't I?

RICHARD

Yes, but they just lie there.

CLAIRE

Hand me one. I'll do one right now. Watch.
   (takes search-a-word book)

RICHARD

Did I tell you I've been taking a self-defense class at the Y? Last night we learned how to disarm a mugger. It's all in the

wrist. You grab them here—
(demonstrates on his wrist)

CLAIRE
(still in search-a-word)
Oh, I just found kumquat!

(KENNY re-enters and goes to CLAIRE's purse.)

KENNY
I need some money for the bus.

RICHARD
Let's show your mother how to disarm a mugger.

KENNY
I'm taking a twenty.
(rummages through purse for money)

RICHARD
Oh no you don't.
(lunges at him with large deliberate moves on each "No!")
No! No! No!
(twists KENNY's wrist hard)

KENNY
Ow! What the hell are you doing?!

RICHARD
Impressive, eh?

KENNY
You could've busted my wrist, ass-wipe!
(picks money off floor)

RICHARD
You don't need that much money for the bus.

KENNY
Quit riding me.

RICHARD
It's chilly. Put on your blue sweater.

KENNY
(to RICHARD*)*
Why can't you just die?!
(exits)

CLAIRE
(nose in search-a-word)
Here's kiwi! It's a fruit-themed puzzle!

RICHARD
He's gonna buy drugs with that money.

CLAIRE
What grade is he in?

RICHARD
Eighth.

CLAIRE
My goodness. He's big for middle school.

RICHARD
He's dyslexic. We're hoping he finally graduates this year.

CLAIRE
(puts down search-a-word)
I'm not sure what's going on exactly.

RICHARD
No, I know. I'm sorry, honey.
(sits next to her)
Uh . . . It's like this: My name is Richard Fiffle, and I'm your
husband.

CLAIRE
You are? My goodness.

RICHARD

Don't be alarmed.

CLAIRE

Who's the boy?

RICHARD

That's your son.

CLAIRE

Really? How much did he weigh at birth?

RICHARD

I don't know, but he loves you very much.

CLAIRE

He's so angry.

RICHARD

He's having a difficult time right now.

CLAIRE

Have I been in a coma of some kind?

RICHARD

No. You have a form of psychogenic amnesia.

CLAIRE

Oh dear, that sounds gruesome. Do go on.

RICHARD

Well, two years ago you woke up one day and your memory
was completely gone.

CLAIRE

How strange.

RICHARD

The doctors assumed it was temporary, but now they're not so
sure.

CLAIRE

Doctors aren't very smart are they?

RICHARD

No, they're not. The strange thing is you're usually very lucid
and capable of understanding complex thoughts. You even re-
tain an enormous amount of information in the course of the
day, but as soon as you go to sleep, it's gone. The next morning we have to start all over again.

CLAIRE

That must be very annoying for you.

RICHARD

Yes, it is.

CLAIRE

So every morning we have the same conversation?

RICHARD

Yes. Well, I change a word here and there, but mostly it's the
same. Sometimes I don't admit it's annoying.

CLAIRE

That's very sweet of you . . . sometimes.

RICHARD
*(grabs what looks like a large filofax from side table
and hands it to her)*
This is a book I designed to get you through your day. I
worked very hard on it.
(turns pages)
See, here's a layout of the house. How the appliances work.
Little photos and descriptions of people you may meet.

CLAIRE

Oh, who is that pathetically sad-looking woman?

RICHARD

That's you, darling.

CLAIRE
No, it can't be! Get me a mirror.

RICHARD
It's an old photo.
(hands her a mirror)
Before you lost your memory.

CLAIRE
(looks at herself in the mirror)
Oh, yes. I look much happier now, Philip.

RICHARD
Richard.

CLAIRE
Right. This photo's too gloomy. Let's get something more chipper.

RICHARD
All right.

CLAIRE
Tell me, *Richard*, if my memory serves me correctly—
(stops and laughs at herself)
Aren't I being ironic?

RICHARD
You make that joke every day.

CLAIRE
Hm. Do you ever laugh?

RICHARD
No.

CLAIRE
How sad. Anyway, if my memory serves me correctly, isn't amnesia usually brought on by some sort of physical or psychological trauma?

RICHARD
(beat)
Uh . . . I'm not sure what you mean.

CLAIRE
I mean something horrible happens and then amnesia kicks in.
Yes, I believe that's correct. I don't know why I remember that.

RICHARD
I need to hop into the shower.

CLAIRE
I don't usually mention trauma, do I?

RICHARD
No. Actually you've *never* mentioned it.

CLAIRE
I could tell by your face that I hadn't. Oh, today *is* a special
day, isn't it?

RICHARD
I'll be in the shower for a little while. I need to be at the hospital for a few hours today.

CLAIRE
But what happened to me?

RICHARD
Small steps, darling. We don't want to exhaust you so early in
the morning.

CLAIRE
Oh, I bet it was unbearable!

RICHARD
The fridge is full. Help yourself.

CLAIRE
Thanks.

RICHARD

Love you.

CLAIRE

Uh . . . okay.

(RICHARD *smiles and exits.*)

CLAIRE
(calls after him)
Hey, what's my name?
(no response)
Richard?
(but he's gone)
So, I have amnesia. Hm, that's very inconvenient.
(beat)
I wonder if I always talk to myself.
(opens the book and reads)
"Good morning, Claire." Claire. Claire. Apparently my name
is Claire.
(reads book again)
"I'm sorry you have no memory." Oh that's very sweet. "To
begin your day, put on your slippers. They are located beside
the bed."
(She sees the slippers.)
Oh, so they are. This is so clever. It's like a little scavenger hunt.
(puts slippers on, then reads)
"Second, take a deep breath and greet the morning."
(she does)
Hello, morning!

(The head of a man *in a ski mask pops out from
under the bed.)*

MAN

Hello, Claire.

CLAIRE

Oh my.

*(The man in the ski mask crawls out from under the
bed. He walks with a limp and speaks with a lisp.)*

LIMPING MAN

Sshhhhh. Don't thay anything.

CLAIRE

Oh dear.

LIMPING MAN

Pleathe, don't be sthcared. I'm thaving you.

CLAIRE

All right.

(The man has a manacle on one wrist, a bit of chain hanging down as if it's been cut.)

LIMPING MAN

You have to come with me.

CLAIRE
(flipping through book)

Hold on, I haven't reached this part yet.

LIMPING MAN

Claire, quickly. While he'th in the shower.

CLAIRE

I'm sorry, this is a little confusing for me.

LIMPING MAN

I'm here to thave you.

CLAIRE
(still with book)

But it doesn't say anything in here about a limping man in a ski mask.

LIMPING MAN

Pleathe, Claire. If you ever loved me, then come with me now.

CLAIRE

Do I know you?

LIMPING MAN

It'th me. Thachary. Your brother. Thachary. Thack! Thacky!

CLAIRE

I have a brother?

LIMPING MAN

Yeth, Claire. Now pleathe, leth sthkedaddle.

CLAIRE

You have such a pronounced lisp.

LIMPING MAN

Yeth, and I altho can't walk properly. I'll exthplain everything later. We've gotta go.

CLAIRE

But I'm in my pajamas.

LIMPING MAN
(grabs dress and some shoes)

That man in the shower ith going to kill you, Claire. He'th a very dangeroth perthon.

CLAIRE

But he seemed so nice.

LIMPING MAN

Leth go, Claire. Pleathe. Come with me.

CLAIRE

Are you gonna take off that mask?

LIMPING MAN

There'th no time.

CLAIRE

Can I take my search-a-word?

LIMPING MAN

Yeth but for godthaykth leth go!

CLAIRE
(grabs puzzle book and filofax)
This is very strange. You do know I have no memory to speak
of?

LIMPING MAN
(rushes her out)
Leth be sthpeedy, Claire. Sthpeedy sthpeedy ethcape. You'll
thank me later.

*(Lights down on the bedroom. Sounds of cars on a
road transition us into—)*

Scene Two

(Lights up in the LIMPING MAN's *car. He's driving.*
CLAIRE *sits beside him.)*

LIMPING MAN
Tho, here we are. Thack and hith thithter. Ith been thuch a
long time, Claire.

CLAIRE
Has it?

LIMPING MAN
Ith very thad whath happened to you.

CLAIRE
Are you gonna take off that mask now?

LIMPING MAN
If you inthitht. But pleathe, don't be thcared.

CLAIRE
Are you deformed?

LIMPING MAN
Yeth. Yeth I am. But only thlightly.

CLAIRE

Ooo, an *unveiling*. I can't wait to see what—

(He pulls off his mask. His right ear is a twisted mass of burnt scar tissue.)

CLAIRE

Ewwwww, your ear is a twisted mass of burnt scar tissue.

LIMPING MAN

Pleathe, try to be a little thenthitive.

CLAIRE

You limp, you lisp, and your ear is all clumpy. What happened to you?

LIMPING MAN

Claire, do you really not remember?

CLAIRE

I'm sorry, I don't.

LIMPING MAN

Good. Ith better you didn't. Thum things are better left forgotten.

CLAIRE

I don't know if that's true.

LIMPING MAN

What?

CLAIRE

I don't know if that's true.

LIMPING MAN

You don't know if *whath* blue?

CLAIRE

True, I said!

LIMPING MAN

Oh. I'm thorry, but whenever you thit on my right like thith, you'll have to thpeak up. I'm deaf in thith ear.

CLAIRE
(yelling into his clumpy ear)
All right!

LIMPING MAN

I'm altho blind in thith eye.

CLAIRE

Should you be driving?

LIMPING MAN

No, but tho long ath they don't catch me, we'll be thuper.

CLAIRE

So long as who doesn't catch you?

LIMPING MAN

Pleathe, you're athking too many quethtions.

CLAIRE

I'm sorry, but that's all I have right now.

LIMPING MAN

Juth look out for the right thide of the car.

CLAIRE

Where are we going again?

LIMPING MAN

To the country. Your mother hath a houth there.

CLAIRE

She does?

LIMPING MAN

Our mother I mean. She'th my mother too, even if she tethti-
fied againtht me, even if she thaid I wath dead to her, she'th
thtill my mother.

CLAIRE

Is she nice?

LIMPING MAN

She had a thtroke rethently and hath trouble forming then-
tentheth properly.

CLAIRE

We're quite a family it seems.

LIMPING MAN

Yeth. Yeth we are.

CLAIRE
(flips through her book)
Does it say anything in here about her?

LIMPING MAN

Put that book away.

CLAIRE
(removes photo from book)
Oh look, here's a photo. "Gertie's House" it says. Mama's name
is Gertie, isn't it? Yes, this house is very familiar. And is that
sweet looking lady Gertie?

LIMPING MAN
(grabs book)
Don't believe anything in thith book, Claire. Ith all lithe. Lithe
that that man made up. Ith garbage.
(throws it out the car window)

CLAIRE

Hey, I needed that book.

LIMPING MAN

You have me now, and I'll tell you everything you need to know.

CLAIRE

All right then, how did I lose my memory?

LIMPING MAN

Exthept that. Your memory problem and the thtory of my phythical infirmiteeth are the two thingth I can't talk about.

CLAIRE

Why are you taking me away like this?

LIMPING MAN

Okay, three thingth, but thath not tho much.

CLAIRE

And why is there a manacle on your wrist?

LIMPING MAN
(getting annoyed)

All right, tho there are many thingth I can't thay right now, but in time everything will be exthplained!

(We hear echoey carnival music far off.)

CLAIRE

Is that your radio playing?

LIMPING MAN

The radio'th buthted.

CLAIRE

Where's that music coming from then?

LIMPING MAN

I don't hear no muthic.

CLAIRE

Ooo, it must be a side-effect of the amnesia. Fun. It's kinda catchy.

*(CLAIRE hums along to the music, then notices
something in the rear-view mirror.)*

CLAIRE

Oh, look at that. I have a little scar on my forehead. How'd I
get that, Zack?

(A very loud horn blares suddenly.)

CLAIRE

Trailer changing lanes! Trailer changing lanes!

LIMPING MAN   CLAIRE
(looking around madly)   *(pointing frantically)*
Where?! Where?!   There! There!

*(He swerves the car. We hear a screech. The trailer
horn fades off.)*

LIMPING MAN

Thank you.

CLAIRE

Maybe *I* should drive.

LIMPING MAN

No, I'm good. We'll be there in no time. Juth relaxth.

CLAIRE

I'm not sure I can at this point, Zack. But I'll try.
(puts photo in her pocket)

*(The lights fade on LIMPING MAN driving, and a
concerned CLAIRE looking around. Again, sounds
of cars transition us into—)*

Scene Three

(Lights up on GERTIE's *kitchen. She's in her 60s, wears a bathrobe, and is sipping tea.* CLAIRE *appears in the kitchen window, looking in at* GERTIE. *She holds up the photo and looks at it, then at* GERTIE, *making sure they're the same.)*

CLAIRE
(at window)
Mama?! You're Mama, right? Mama, it's me. Your daughter Claire. I have amnesia.

GERTIE
Clay? Whadda dune hay? Youshen be gnome!

CLAIRE
I hear you've had a stroke. That's terrible.

GERTIE
Income, Clay. Income!

CLAIRE
Did you know I was traumatized and no one will tell me what happened?

GERTIE
(waving her in)
Income, Clay. In . . . come . . . in . . . come in.

CLAIRE
Oh, all right.

(The LIMPING MAN *appears at the window.* GERTIE's *surprised and unhappy to see him.)*

LIMPING MAN
Hello, Mama. Did you mith me?

CLAIRE
Look, Mama, it's Zack! Are you surprised? I was too. But he was wearing a mask when I saw him, so it was surprising *and* scary at the same time.

GERTIE
(to LIMPING MAN*)*
Fee, whadda helen oodoo?

CLAIRE
He's apparently saving me from Richard Fiffle.

LIMPING MAN
I know you're not happy to thee me.

GERTIE
Dashen dunder-mince-tate.

CLAIRE
Zack was saying you two didn't get along.

LIMPING MAN
But I'm juth thtaying a couple hourth, Mama, and I'll be on my betht behavior if you thtay on yourth. Okay?

GERTIE
Income, Clay.

CLAIRE
(to LIMPING MAN*)*
That means "come in" in stroke talk.

LIMPING MAN
We'll come around the front. I remember the way.

CLAIRE
See ya' in a sec!

(CLAIRE *and* LIMPING MAN *leave window and go around front.* GERTIE *collects herself. She grabs a knife from a drawer, places it within reach, and throws a dish-towel over it to hide it.*

LIMPING MAN *and* CLAIRE *enter the kitchen.)*

                    CLAIRE
        (happy to see her)
Mama!

                    GERTIE
Clay!
        (hugs CLAIRE*)*

                LIMPING MAN
Jeeth Loueeth, thith kitchen hathn't changed a bit. Ith like a
mutheum.

                    CLAIRE
I think it's a pretty house. I can tell I grew up here.

                LIMPING MAN
        (grabs dusty old baseball mitt from top of fridge)
Hey, my old baseball glove!

                    CLAIRE
I feel like I've come home to the bosom of my Mama.

                LIMPING MAN
You know what I like about it? The theclusion. Privathy ith
pritheleth.

                    CLAIRE
        (looks out the window)
What a huge tree.
        (to LIMPING MAN*)*
Did you climb it?

                LIMPING MAN
What?

                    CLAIRE
When you were little? You used to climb that tree all the time.
Right? Higher and higher?

LIMPING MAN

(beat)
Yeah. I did. Right, Gertie?

CLAIRE

See? I remember some things. Don't tell me I don't remember things.

GERTIE

Fast break?

CLAIRE

What?

GERTIE

Fast break, Clay? Eggs? Sear-el? Toe-sat? Fast break?

CLAIRE

Breakfast?

GERTIE

Fast break, Clay?

CLAIRE

I'd love some. We just ran out this morning and didn't have any time to stop and eat.

(GERTIE *opens up the freezer door.*)

GERTIE

Balcony?

CLAIRE

No, I don't think I want baloney, Mama.

GERTIE

(holds up bacon)
Balcony?

LIMPING MAN

No! Goddamit, no bacon! Never bacon! Never make bacon!

(throws bacon out the window)
You *know* I don't like bacon, Gertie.

CLAIRE

(pause)
I think you should apologize. You scared Mama.

LIMPING MAN

I'm thorry. I don't . . . like . . . bacon.

GERTIE

I jez hava fidful oh da balcony cuz ya foddeh lie dit so moo, I
jez godden haboo oh keeboo da-roun oda tie.

CLAIRE

Hmmm. That's a very good story, Mama.

LIMPING MAN

You have a hack-thaw, Mom?

GERTIE

Hack?

LIMPING MAN

Yeah, I have thomething to do.

GERTIE

Ina la.

LIMPING MAN

What?

GERTIE

La.

LIMPING MAN

La?

CLAIRE

In the cellar, she said. Daddy's workbench is against the back wall. And there are some saws hanging to the left. There's a hack-saw with a red handle.

LIMPING MAN
(beat)
Thankth, Claire.
(exits into basement)

CLAIRE
This house is so nice, Mama. I know things about it. It's good for me, right?

GERTIE
Clay . . .

CLAIRE
Did they tell you I lose my memory every day? That must be a very rare thing.
(inhales deeply)
Oh I think I can still smell Daddy's cologne. It must've seeped into the wallpaper.

GERTIE
I doan tink toe, Clay.
(checks that LIMPING MAN's *out of earshot)*

CLAIRE
(straining to remember)
Yes, I think I can picture him. Did he wear a yellow cap?

GERTIE
Clay, lessco fo wah, kay?

CLAIRE
Hold on. There used to be cages out back, weren't there? With dogs in them. And Daddy would feed them in the morning.

GERTIE
Isso ny ow sigh, lessco fo wah.

CLAIRE

He'd line up all those dog dishes and fill them with kibble, and
I'd help him carry them out to the cages. You and Dad ran a
kennel.

GERTIE

Ya, da kenny. Buh Clay, lissa toe-me, peas.

CLAIRE

And Daddy would walk all the dogs at once. Seven or eight at
a time. All these leashes pulling in different directions. And
he'd come over that hill looking like a map of the universe.
Yeah, Daddy's yellow hat was the sun and he had all these dog
planets revolving around him. And on the longest leash was
Mrs. Paulson's terrier, Chippy. And Chippy was like the planet
Pluto, because he was so far away from Daddy and so little.
How long ago was that, Mama? I must've been about ten.

(A homemade hand puppet, equipped with little
arms in little manacles, appears in the window.)

PUPPET
(goofy voice)
Hellooooo beautiful ladies. My name is Hinky Binky. Can I be
your friend?

CLAIRE
(beat)
Well this is very strange, isn't it?

PUPPET

I've got an itch on the top of my head that I can't reach. It's
driving me craaaaaazyyy!

CLAIRE

Who are you?

PUPPET

I'm Hinky Binky. Scratch my head.

CLAIRE

Is this normal, Mama?

PUPPET

Scratch my itch, bitch!

CLAIRE

Excuse me, but you're not being very nice.

PUPPET

Nice bites, right Millet?
            (MILLET's *normal voice*)
Don't say my name.
            (*puppet voice*)
Why can't I say your name, *Millet*?
            (*normal*)
You're gonna get me in trouble!
            (*puppet singing*)
Miiiiilllllleeeeettttttt . . . Milllleeeettttttt.

            (*A gristled man stands up, the puppet on his hand.
            He strangles the puppet.*)

MILLET

Cut it out! You gotta remember the rules!
            (*realizes that he's been seen*)
Ahh!

            (CLAIRE *and* GERTIE *scream when he screams. He
            disappears again.*)

CLAIRE

What a crazy puppet man. Do you know him, Mama?

GERTIE

No, Clay. Ida know no puppas!

            (LIMPING MAN *runs in with hacksaw.*)

LIMPING MAN

Wath that Millet?

CLAIRE

You know him?

LIMPING MAN

Where'd he go?

CLAIRE

He scared us.

(*The puppet appears again at the window.*)

PUPPET

I'm Hinky Binky with the two-foot dinky.

CLAIRE

What a filthy puppet.

LIMPING MAN

Millet!

(LIMPING MAN *grabs puppet and pulls it off the puppet man's hand, revealing that he too has a manacle on his wrist.*)

MILLET
(*still with puppet voice*)
Yikes, now I'm just a hand. Boo hoo hoo!

LIMPING MAN

I thought we talked about this?

(MILLET *stands in window, shamefaced.*)

MILLET

I'm sorry.

LIMPING MAN

Didn't we talk about thith?

MILLET

Yes. Can I have my puppet back?

LIMPING MAN

You frightened the women.

MILLET

I'm real sorry, ladies.

LIMPING MAN

He didn't mean nothing by it. Milleth okay.
(hands him puppet)

MILLET

Thank you.
(puts it back on)
I feel much better.

LIMPING MAN

Thith ith Claire.

MILLET

Nice to meet you, ma'am.

LIMPING MAN

And thath Gertie.

MILLET

(as puppet)
Like a hurdy-gurdy? If I turn your crank, will you play?

(MILLET *and* LIMPING MAN *laugh at the puppet's
strange joke.*)

CLAIRE

You both have manacles on. Did you escape from a chain
gang?

(They stop laughing.)

LIMPING MAN

You should juth know, Claire, that everything I do, I do for
you.

MILLET

We gonna cut this cuff off?
    (as puppet)
Please cut it off. I'm gonna go craaaaazyyy.

LIMPING MAN

We got a vithe in the bathement. That'll hold 'em in plathe.
You come around the front.

MILLET

    (as puppet)
I'll be there in two shakes!
    (goes around front)

LIMPING MAN

Now you both be nithe to Millet. Hith mother wath a free-
bather.

CLAIRE

A what?

LIMPING MAN

A *free*bather

    (CLAIRE *still doesn't get it.*)

GERTIE

A base-freezer, Clay. Day base-freeze croquet.

CLAIRE

Oh. I love croquet. I was always the blue mallet.
    (laughs—those were good times)

    (Now it's GERTIE *and* LIMPING MAN *who are confused.*

    MILLET *strolls in, wearing a stolen suit with the
    price tags and security tags still attached.)*

MILLET

Sorry I'm late. I stopped by J.C. Penney to pick this up.
(indicates suit, then notices the kitchen)
Wow, this is so weird. Because one time—
(cheery puppet)
Millet was sodomized in a house like this.

LIMPING MAN

Hey!

MILLET

Sorry. He's not used to being around ladies.

LIMPING MAN

Did you get everything on the list?

MILLET

Yeah, it's all in the trunk of my car.

CLAIRE

Did you steal those cars?

MILLET

Yeah, we did!

LIMPING MAN

Millet—

MILLET

(realizes)
Oh, I mean . . . we made them.

CLAIRE

And the manacles . . . You guys used to be attached?

MILLET

Yeah. They chain us together when we work in the kitchen.

LIMPING MAN

What I thay about talking?

MILLET

Oops. You said don't say too much at the *rendezvous*.

CLAIRE

This is a rendezvous?

LIMPING MAN
(to MILLET*)*
You thee what happenth? More quethtionth.

MILLET

I won't say anything else.

LIMPING MAN

Now leth go to the bathement.

MILLET
(sings as puppet)
And then we'll shuffle off to Buffalo.

(LIMPING MAN *and* MILLET *exit into basement.)*

CLAIRE

Life can be so funny, Mama.

GERTIE

Clay, noo-noo dish is gooey.

CLAIRE

What's the matter?

GERTIE

Ees med ah noose bah.

CLAIRE

We need a dictionary for you. A translation book.

GERTIE

Clay, dish is nah—

(LIMPING MAN *re-enters.)*

LIMPING MAN

Claire, come talk to me and Millet in the bathement. I haven't theen you in tho long. You can talk to Mama any old time.

CLAIRE

That puppet's got a potty mouth, Philip.

LIMPING MAN

Thack.

CLAIRE

Right. Zack. What'd I say?

LIMPING MAN

I'll tell him to thtop with the puppet. Milleth not too bright, but he lithenth.

CLAIRE

All right then. Mama, do you mind? I've never spent any time with criminals before.

LIMPING MAN

You know that for thertain, Claire?
    (laughs at his joke)

CLAIRE

Oh, right. I get it. I lost my memory, so—

LIMPING MAN

We'll be doing handiwork, Gertie.

> (LIMPING MAN *and* CLAIRE *go to basement.* GERTIE *goes to the phone and dials 911.)*

GERTIE
    (into phone)
Isis Geht Maso. Fee cape. Eesh ina hiss . . . Huh? . . .
    (They don't understand her; she clarifies.)
Fee cape . . . *Cape* . . . Ee brogue adder summer . . . *Fee cape!*
. . . Geht Maso! . . . *Fee cape!!!*

(LIMPING MAN *re-enters. He forgot something.* GERTIE
quickly tries to look like she's making small talk.)

GERTIE
(into phone)
Ish da rye? Dah isho fuddy.

LIMPING MAN
Who are you talking to, Gertie?

GERTIE
(into phone)
Hoe-down do sicken.
(to LIMPING MAN*)*
Iyas mah frient . . . I cull mah frient . . . thall.

LIMPING MAN
(hangs the phone up)
How bout we keep quiet? No calling people. No blabbing to
Claire. Juth quiet time, okay?

GERTIE
No Fee, yoda ony baddy doo Clay.

LIMPING MAN
You mention anything and I'll kill you, Gertie. I thwear to God,
I'll cut off your fuckin head and *bury you in THE BACK YARD!!!*

(silence)

LIMPING MAN
I'm thorry. You juth . . . Leth be normal, okay?
(apologetically)
Really, I'm trying to . . . You want thum candy?
(pulls candy from pockets and lays it on table)
Here, have thum candy. Thee? I can be good, Mama. Watch.
I'll juth thit here and be good while you make breakfatht. Like
in the old dayth. They don't need me down there. I can be
good, Mama. I *can* be.

*(Lights down on the kitchen. The sound of some-
one scanning a car radio transitions us into—)*

Scene Four

(Lights up inside car. RICHARD *drives.* KENNY *is smoking a joint and scanning the car radio.)*

RICHARD
Kenny, can you please just pick a station and stay there?

*(*KENNY *stops on a 70's easy-listening song.)*

KENNY
Sweet.
(leans back and takes a hit from his joint)

RICHARD
You know, most fathers wouldn't allow their kids to smoke marijuana in the car. I hope you appreciate how understanding I'm trying to be.

KENNY
Why did you pick me up at the bus stop? I said I didn't need a ride.

*(*RICHARD *clicks off the radio.)*

KENNY
Hey, I was listening to that.

RICHARD
Kenny, listen to me. Your mother is missing.

KENNY
Huh.
(takes another hit)

RICHARD
You gotta help me be the search party. Keep your eyes open, she could be anywhere.

*(*KENNY *exhales pot smoke)*

RICHARD

Hey, blow it that way. I'm getting a contact buzz.

KENNY

So wait, she just wandered off?

RICHARD

She was acting a little strange this morning.

KENNY

Maybe she finally wised up and ran away from your nutty ass.

RICHARD

I love your mother, Kenny. Very much. I know you harbor some animosity for me, but I've tried to be a good husband and a good father, and if I've misplaced your mother, I've lost everything.

KENNY

You know what I hear when you talk? "Kenny, blah-blah-bloo-pity-bloop."

RICHARD

I can tell you're upset. Well, you know what? Don't even think of this as a search party. Just think of it as a drive in the car. This is what families do. They go for drives. You wanna play "I Spy"?

KENNY

Are you retarded?

RICHARD

Okay, I'm hearing that you're angry. And the pot tells me you're trying to dull the pain at the center of your life.

KENNY

(snickers)
The road is all wobbly.

RICHARD

But I know the siren-call of ganja, Kenny. They used to call me Maryjane McGee. Or Cannabis Carl. Or J.P. Toke-Meister.

KENNY
(staring intently at his hand)
Hands can look like spiders.

RICHARD
But it leads to other things. Terrible, damaging things. I know.
I used to have a very serious drug problem. You should learn
from my mistakes like other children.

KENNY
Other children learn from your mistakes?

RICHARD
What? You're stoned.
   (beat)
Wanna play "I Went on a Picnic"?

KENNY
I bet if I had bionic eyes we could find her really quick.

RICHARD
I think she's hitchhiking to your grandmother's.

KENNY
Why do you think that?

RICHARD
   (holds up her book)
I found her book on the road and the only thing missing from
it is the photo of Gertie's house.

KENNY
Weird.
   (looks out the window)
Oh my god, that van-load of kids is staring at me. Look at
them. They're all staring right through me. It's wiggin' me out.

RICHARD
Ah yes, the paranoia. For a long time I thought there were
people after me too. But that's because I did something very

bad, and I've never paid for it, so I was always waiting for the other foot to drop. But it never did. And I pray it never will.

(*Silence as* KENNY *stares at him.*)

RICHARD

I'm sorry. I'm feeling a little off-kilter today. I hope we find your mother soon. Otherwise I—I don't what I'm gonna— May I have a hit?

KENNY

What?

RICHARD

Just a little one. To take the edge off.

(KENNY *passes him the joint. Richard takes a hit.*)

RICHARD
(*holding breath in*)
I really shouldn't be doing this, but I'm worried about your mom and—
(*suddenly*)
Did I ever tell you about the time I met Dennis Hopper?

(*A siren blares in distance.*)

RICHARD

Aw geez, it's the fuzz.
(*tosses joint out the window*)
Open the windows. Air it out.
(*pulls over*)
See what happens, Kenny? Drugs lead to crime. Let that be a lesson. Try and act natural.
(*waits for cop*)
Jeepers. I get awful jumpy around the pigs. How are my eyes? Bloodshot?

KENNY

Shut up, moron.

(HEIDI, *a cop, approaches.*)

RICHARD

How-do, officer?

HEIDI

In a hurry this morning?

RICHARD

Not especially. I'm just out for a drive with the boy, playing some "I Spy," heading to the Friendly's for a treat.

HEIDI

Kinda early for a Fribble, isn't it?

RICHARD

Not for this family. We love ice cream. Right, Kenny?

HEIDI

I clocked you going eighty-four in a fifty-five zone.

RICHARD

Is that right? Well, I'll be. Maybe that speedy-radar thingy of yours needs new batteries.

(KENNY *gets a giggle-fit which may last through the scene.*)

HEIDI

Have you been smoking marijuana in this vehicle, sir?

RICHARD

No ma'am I have not.

HEIDI

Smells like maybe someone was, sir.

RICHARD

Well, Kenny here, I must admit was toking up a bit of the doobage, so to speak.

HEIDI

I'll be needing your license and registration, sir, and then I'd like you both to step out of the vehicle.

RICHARD

Oh, you misunderstood me. You see, Kenny here has glaucoma and he smokes pot for purely medicinal purposes.

HEIDI

And do you have a letter from your doctor stating as much?

RICHARD

Actually, our doctor had a terrible accident and he no longer has hands, so writing a note isn't possible for him right now. But as soon as he's fitted for prosthetic limbs and learns how to write with those awkward little hooks I'll pass the note onto the highway patrol office.

HEIDI

I believe you're lying to me, sir.

RICHARD

No, he was fiddling inside a lawn mower in between operations and—

HEIDI

Sir?

RICHARD

All right, I'm lying. But Kenny here is a troubled teen and— Fritos! I suddenly want Fritos! Are you craving Fritos, Kenny?
        (snickers)

KENNY

Mmmmm. Fritos.

HEIDI

        (pulls gun on him)
Please step out of the vehicle, sir!

RICHARD

Hold on there, flat-foot. I don't think we need you pulling a Rodney King here.

HEIDI

Get out of the car!

RICHARD

Okay. We're getting out, but this is all much ado about nothing, eh Kenny?

(They step out of car, HEIDI's *gun on them.* KENNY *is trying not to giggle.)*

HEIDI

License and registration please.

RICHARD
(hands them over)

This is all very unnecessary, officer. You see, my wife has a form of psychogenic amnesia, and she wandered off this morning . . .

HEIDI

I think I've heard just about enough of your stories, tough guy.

RICHARD

Tough guy? I'm not tough guy. I'm *nice* guy. Everyone I know calls me *nice* guy.

HEIDI
(looking at license)

Well, Mr. *Fiffle*, if that's your *real* name, I'm gonna radio back to headquarters and have them pop your name into a computer and see what turns up.

RICHARD

Headquarters? Computer? No! No! No!

(He goes into self-defense mode, lunging at her with each "No!" He twists her wrist so she drops the gun. He scrambles for it and points it at her.)

RICHARD

Well, the shoe's on the other hand now, isn't it, copper?

HEIDI

Sir, I am a police officer, which means you need to return my revolver.

RICHARD

I'm sorry, but that isn't possible. You see, I have a very complicated past and can't afford your popping my name into any computer. So I'm afraid you're gonna have to come with us.

KENNY

You're gonna get us thrown in jail, shit-for-brains.

RICHARD

You know what, Kenny? I wish you'd stop calling me names. It hurts my feelings.

HEIDI

Sir, why don't you just head on home, I'll forget I stopped you and we'll call it a day.

RICHARD

Because I have to find my wife! It's only been a couple hours and look at me!

HEIDI

Sir, let's not get excited.

RICHARD

Everyone back in the car!

(*Lights out on them. The 70's easy-listening song transitions us into* —)

Scene Five

(The basement. There's a workbench with a vise nearby, as well as several boxes filled with old toys and junk. MILLET's *manacle has been cut off and sits on the workbench with a few old dolls. As the lights come up,* CLAIRE *is jumping rope.* MILLET *is trying to hula hoop. They sing a children's song together.* MILLET *sings as the puppet.)*

CLAIRE AND MILLET
Cinderella, dressed in yella.
Went downstairs to kiss a fella.
Made a mistake and kissed a snake.
How many doctors did it take?
One. Two. Three. Four—

*(*CLAIRE *messes up and stops skipping rope.* MILLET *stops hula hooping.)*

MILLET
(puppet)
Four! It took four doctors!

(They laugh together, giddy.)

CLAIRE
Isn't it fun down here?

MILLET
Yeah.
(suddenly notices a nearby kewpie doll)
Except for that doll. It's kinda creepy. Face it the other way, okay?

CLAIRE
(picks up kewpie doll)
Oh, look at that. I bet someone won it for me. I bet my Dad knocked down a stack of milk bottles with one shot! Whaddaya think?

MILLET

I think maybe you weren't supposed to go through that stuff.

CLAIRE

Why?

MILLET

I . . . I should tell Zack I cut off my manacle.
(heads for stairs)

CLAIRE

(cuts him off at the pass)
Hold on, Millet. He's busy making up with Mama.

MILLET

Yeah, but I don't like basements.

CLAIRE

Oh come on, we're having so much fun.

MILLET

(puppet)
And you didn't cut off *my* manacles!
(normal)
But Binky—
(puppet)
I'm gettin' all squirrelly! Now cut 'em off!
(normal)
Okay! Stop yelling!
(to CLAIRE)
Binky's got little manacles too.

CLAIRE

Yeah. I saw that. Cute.

MILLET

Thanks.

(MILLET puts BINKY's tiny manacle in the vise and begins sawing it off.)

CLAIRE
Do you think they're talking about me up there?

MILLET
I . . . I don't know.

CLAIRE
Sure you don't know.
(pulls monster mask from box)
Look. I bet it was Zack's. I bet he'd wear it and scare me and make me scream.
(laughs at mask)

MILLET
It gives me the willies. Put it away, okay?

CLAIRE
You're such a Nervous Nellie.

MILLET
Hey, where'd you get that ring?

CLAIRE
(notices it for the first time)
Oh. I don't know.

MILLET
Principal Leone had a ring just like that.

CLAIRE
Who's Principal Leone?

MILLET
My old boss. I used to be janitor at a grade school.

CLAIRE
Is that right?

MILLET
And Principal Leone had a ring just like that. Hers had a nice

diamond in the middle and two rubies on the side. Every morning I would say "Hello Principal Leone. That's a very pretty ring."
    (puppet)
Stupid whore wrecked your life!
    (normal)
She fired me.

CLAIRE

Why'd she do that?

MILLET

Oh, I . . . I'm not supposed to—

CLAIRE

Come on, you can talk about *yourself*. He just told you to not say anything about *me*, right?

MILLET

She . . . She said I scared the children. I would growl at them and chase them with my pail of sawdust for fun. And she said I scared the children.

CLAIRE

I'm sorry, Millet.

MILLET

And the next day, when I woke up, there were two cops standing over my bed. And they said I beat up Principal Leone in the parking lot and stole her ring. Which was very surprising to me. I mean, in court I had to admit that I had just been fired, and yes I had said I liked her ring, and it was true that often I have blackouts, but I'm not a violent person.

CLAIRE

So, that's how you ended up in prison? You stole a ring?

MILLET

I guess so.

CLAIRE
And that's where you met Zack?

MILLET
Yeah, in the yard.

CLAIRE
Oh, the *yard*. It sounds so rough. Was he lifting weights?

MILLET
No. This lifer named Twitchy was threatening Binky with a shiv.
(*puppet*)
So I squeezed his nuts and made him cry!
(*normal*)
But then the guards started shooting at us from the towers, and Zack pushed us out of the way of the bullets. So we became friends. He likes to talk to me.

CLAIRE
Oh yeah? Does he ever say anything about me?

MILLET
Sure. He calls you his little blank thlate.

CLAIRE
Really? Does he ever say *why* I'm his little blank thlate?

MILLET
Uhh . . . I'm not really allowed to talk about it.

CLAIRE
Oh, right.

MILLET
It's just . . . he has these plans—

CLAIRE
Plans?

MILLET

And he made me promise not to say too much, which is hard for me, because when I get nervous, I just jabber on.

CLAIRE

Why are you nervous?

MILLET

(as puppet)
Millet's a chicken-shit!
(laughs at BINKY)
I just don't like basements.
(as puppet)
Plus *I've* got a biiiiiiiigggg mouth!
(normal)
Yeah, I'm a little afraid of Binky getting me in trouble.

CLAIRE

Well, he hasn't said anything too damaging yet.

MILLET

(as puppet)
Give it time, bitch!

CLAIRE

I wish he didn't have such a foul mouth.

MILLET

Yeah, me too.

CLAIRE

Where'd you get him anyway?

MILLET

I made him. A lady from the church came into the prison and showed us how.
(puppet)
Fuckin' nuns, I hate them!
(normal)
Sorry. Catholic school.

CLAIRE

Oh, you're Catholic.

MILLET

Not me. Just Binky.

CLAIRE

Oh.
(pulls squirt gun from box)
Look, squirt gun! It's so funny, Gertie saved all our toys.

(As CLAIRE holds up the squirt gun, we hear a dog barking, far off, echoey. She looks around, disoriented.)

CLAIRE

Did you hear that?

MILLET

What?

CLAIRE

The dog. You didn't hear a dog barking?
(taps her head with the palm of her hand)

MILLET

No. You okay?

CLAIRE

Yeah, I just . . . I'm fine.

(CLAIRE puts the squirt gun down. MILLET returns to sawing his cuff.)

CLAIRE

I'd tell *you*, you know.

MILLET

What?

CLAIRE

If I knew what happened during those blackouts of yours and you wanted to know, I'd tell you.

MILLET

I can't. I'm just here to saw my manacle. I'm sorry.

CLAIRE
(playful)
Oh. You're sorry?
(puts on mask, silly monster voice)
Millet's sorry he can't talk about Claire's amnesia.

(MILLET *laughs nervously.*)

CLAIRE
(creeps to him, monster voice)
Well, what if I *made* you talk about it?
(points squirt gun at him)

MILLET

I thought you were gonna put that away?

CLAIRE
(threatening monster voice)
What if I tortured you until you *had* to talk about it?

(*She puts down squirt gun, and grabs the saw from him.*)

MILLET

Hey.

CLAIRE
(grabs MILLET's *arm)*
What if I said I'd cut off your hand if you didn't tell me about my amnesia?!

MILLET
(petrified)
That's my puppet hand.

CLAIRE

Tell me what happened, Millet!

MILLET

Please!

CLAIRE

Tell me!

MILLET

I can't!

CLAIRE

(whips off mask)
Kidding!

(She screams with laughter. He just stares at her, frightened.)

CLAIRE

What's the matter?
(pause)
I wasn't really gonna do it. I'm not like that, Millet. I don't have it in me.

MILLET

(beat)
Yes you do.

CLAIRE

(pause)
What's that supposed to mean?

MILLET

Nothing. I promised I wouldn't—
(puppet interrupts)
Your husband threw the Empire State Building at your forehead.

CLAIRE

(beat)
What'd he say?

MILLET
(puppet)
It was a souvenir paperweight!
(normal)
Binky—

CLAIRE
(touches the scar on her forehead)
Is that what this is?

MILLET
(puppet)
Another time he got mad because you said his shirt was a girly
shirt—
(normal)
You know we're not—
(puppet)
As a joke you said it, but he got mad!
(normal)
I promised!
(puppet)
And he threw you across the floor and poured a bowl of cereal
on you and slammed your head against the oven door and you
were unconscious for three hours!
(normal)
Stop it, Binky!
(rips puppet off his hand)
There. Sorry. Please don't tell him Binky said anything. He'll
be so mad.

CLAIRE
Is that why my brother took me away? Because Richard Fiffle beat me up?

MILLET
I don't know! I don't know anything!

*(Again, we hear the echoey dog barking, louder
this time. CLAIRE taps her head.)*

CLAIRE
Goddamit! You don't hear barking?!

MILLET

I hate basements!

(LIMPING MAN *enters from upstairs.*)

LIMPING MAN

Hey, kidth. Everyone playing nithe?

CLAIRE

Why didn't you tell me Richard Fiffle poured cereal on me?

LIMPING MAN

Oh. Millet mentioned that?

MILLET

It was the puppet.

LIMPING MAN

Thingth can get tho complicated, Claire. And I have tho much
to do today.

CLAIRE

Still . . .

LIMPING MAN

I can't exthplain everything to you and do everything elth, and
then have you go to thleep and do it all over again tomorrow.
I'm prethed for time.

CLAIRE

But he said you had a plan and—

LIMPING MAN

Forget everything Millet thed. Leth juth have a *nithe* day.
Okay?

CLAIRE

But my head's all jumbled and I'm hearing barking and music
and—

LIMPING MAN

You're thafe, Claire. You don't need to get all worked up about who'th who or whath what. Your brother hath taken you away from the bad man. Thath all you need to know. I'm gonna take care of you. From now on, it'll be nothing but eathy chairth and warm baked goodth. Okay?

CLAIRE

Okay.
    (smiles)
Thank you, Zack.

LIMPING MAN

Sure.

    (She kisses him on the cheek, but he turns his head,
    planting a kiss on her lips. It lands a little too
    firmly and lasts a little too long.)

CLAIRE
    (pause)
Is our family always so friendly?

LIMPING MAN

Go have thum breakfatht. Your mom'th waiting for you. *Our* mom, I mean. *Our* mom.

CLAIRE
    (uneasily)
Uhh . . . Okay.
    (exits)

MILLET

She had a monster mask and a weird voice and you know I don't like basements. And she said she was gonna cut off my hand and—

LIMPING MAN
    (picks up hacksaw)
Thtop thpeaking, Millet. I don't wanna hear you thpeak right now.
    (saws his cuff)

MILLET
You shouldn't have left me alone for so long.

LIMPING MAN
Didn't I thay don't thpeak?

MILLET
Yeah.

LIMPING MAN
All right then.

MILLET
(side of the mouth, as puppet)
Can I speak?

LIMPING MAN
No. Leth jutht get thith done.

(Lights fade on LIMPING MAN *sawing cuff. Sounds of cars transition us into—)*

Scene Six

(Lights up on RICHARD's *car.* KENNY *has the gun pointed at* HEIDI, *who's seated between him and* RICHARD *in the front seat.* HEIDI *is nervous, but tries to look calm.)*

RICHARD
Now remember, Kenny, once we get there, don't let your mom know we were worried. We can't upset her. Everything's good. Smile a lot when you see her.

KENNY
If she's there, you mean.

RICHARD
Oh she'll be there. She *has* to be there.

HEIDI

We just crossed the state line, in case you're keeping track of the felonies you're racking up.

RICHARD

See, this is no good. I've kidnapped a lady cop.

HEIDI

My name's Heidi.

RICHARD

I've kidnapped Heidi. You see why I need your mother? This is the old me. You're in a car with the old me. Can you tell?

KENNY

I don't even know what the hell you're talking about.

RICHARD

I try to be a good man. I get a good job at the hospital. Get a good family. And then one morning it's all gone. I'm back where I started, smokin' reefer, kidnappin' cops, crossin' state lines. It just shows ya' that stability is a fragile figurine.
    (beat)
Maybe Polly Harkness was right. I'm just a know-nothin' druggie, and that's all I'll ever be.

KENNY

Who's Polly Harkness?

RICHARD

No one! And never mention her name again!
    (turns to HEIDI suddenly)
I love my wife so much. You understand, don't you? You ever been married?

HEIDI

Three times.

RICHARD

Wow. Didn't work out, huh? Husbands were no good?

HEIDI
(ignores his question)
You can still turn around, you know.

RICHARD
Some women are just *drawn* to bad apples. Was that you?

HEIDI
Did I mention there was a camera mounted on my dashboard?

RICHARD
I didn't see any camera.

HEIDI
It's very small. Records all my pull-overs. Picks up license plates real clear.

RICHARD
Quit trying to scare me!

HEIDI
(trying to sound tough)
Well, you *should* be scared because you're in for it, buster!

RICHARD
Buster? You people actually use that word?

HEIDI
Yes, we use many words. It's hot in here. Can you roll down a window? Are you hot? I'm getting very hot.

RICHARD
You seem awful nervous for a cop.

HEIDI
Yeah, well, I've got a gun in my face.

RICHARD
We won't use it, so long as you don't try anything. I just wanna find my wife and clear my name.

HEIDI

I said I'd forget about it if you let me go.

KENNY

Pull over, butt-munch. She said she'd forget about it.

RICHARD

That's just a cop trick, Kenny. They are wily, wily creatures.

HEIDI

I bet your wife's at home. I bet someone found her and brought her home.

RICHARD

On the outside Heidi seems to make sense, but underneath, she's crazy. Crazy like a fox.

KENNY

It's like you're underwater to me. Blah-blah-bloopity-bloop.

RICHARD

(to HEIDI)
Aren't they cute at this age?

KENNY

Don't patronize me, douche-bag.

RICHARD

Kenny and I have some issues to work out. Can you tell?

HEIDI

Sir, I'm losing my patience.

RICHARD

Kenny, you're the navigator. Read me the road signs.

KENNY

I'm dyslexic, moron.

HEIDI
My husbands were not bad apples.

(KENNY *lights up another joint.*)

RICHARD
Kenny, don't you light up in here.

HEIDI
They were troubled, but that certainly wasn't something I was drawn to.

RICHARD
You are not gonna be all glassy-eyed when we meet your mother.

KENNY
Bite me.

RICHARD
I try to be fatherly to this kid—

HEIDI
Open the window! I'm hot and claustrophobic!

RICHARD
We need to have an intervention here.

HEIDI
I'm starting to feel like the car is shrinking.

RICHARD
I'm intervening!
        (*grabs joint and throws it out the window*)

KENNY
Hey!

(HEIDI *is hyperventilating.*)

RICHARD
I love you, Kenny. Heidi and I are here for you. We love you
and support you.

KENNY
You make me wanna puke!

RICHARD
That's it, Kenny! I am so sick of your pissy wise-ass comments!
You can go fuck yourself, you miserable little prick!

(KENNY *is visibly stung.*)

RICHARD
There! How do *you* like it?

HEIDI
Jesus, I'm sweatin' like a Mexican whore!

RICHARD
(offended)
Hey, watch it! My mother's half-Mexican.

HEIDI
I gotta unbutton my shirt.

RICHARD
That uniform looks too big for you. Didn't they have one your
size?

HEIDI
I wear my clothes baggy.

RICHARD
Well it's not flattering. You should wear something that fits.

HEIDI
I'll give you something that fits when I shove my billy-club up
your ass and slap you around like a piñata!

RICHARD
You see, Kenny? The cop shows her true colors. The mask has slipped!

HEIDI
You're pissing me off and I'm claustrophobic and I don't wanna go to the country! Turn this fucking car around!

(KENNY has put the gun in his mouth.)

KENNY
I'm gonna kill myself!

RICHARD
You think that's funny?!

HEIDI
Don't drool on my piece, nimrod!

RICHARD
What has your mother said about playing with guns?

KENNY
(takes gun out)
Doesn't anyone *care?!*

RICHARD
Of course we care.
(suddenly distracted)
Oh look, a Denny's! I love that place.

HEIDI
(also pleased)
Oooo.

(He swerves and screeches as he makes the exit. Lights out on them. The echoey carnival music transitions us into—)

Scene Seven

(Lights up on GERTIE'*s kitchen.* GERTIE *is buzzing around, searching for something.* CLAIRE *sits at the table doing a search-a-word puzzle.)*

CLAIRE

That puppet was saying the craziest things about me. Is he a trustworthy source of information?

GERTIE

Trush noon by me, Clay.

CLAIRE

Okay.
(returns to search a word)
Oh, I just found banana.
(circles it)
What are you looking for?

GERTIE

Dusha riddle dimsum da my hempoo.
(rushes off to another part of the house)

CLAIRE

You need any help?

GERTIE

(off)
I doan tink-toe!

(We hear one echoey bark. CLAIRE *looks up. It suddenly comes to her.)*

CLAIRE

Nancy! Oh, I just got the bark! Mr. Cuthart's old retriever. Thank god. It was on the tip of my brain all morning. I just remembered something, Mama!

GERTIE

(off)
Dash ny!

CLAIRE
(back to puzzle book)
Oh, and here's cantaloupe! I'm on a roll!

(CLAIRE circles word. GERTIE enters, still searching.)

CLAIRE
You remember that dog? Skinny old thing Mr. Cuthart kept
tied up in the front lawn all day? Daddy always said he was
gonna report him. Remember she just sat in the sun, biting at
her scabs? Cuthart didn't even give her any water.

GERTIE
Who do teching bat?

CLAIRE
Nancy. So I'd sneak down the road with my squirt gun, and
spritz water into her mouth, and she'd bark.

GERTIE
Uh-huh. I bee rye bag.
(rushes off to another part of the house)

CLAIRE
And one day, when Cuthart was downtown, I untied her to let
her run around a little. But she darted straight into the road,
just as Daddy's pick-up was coming around the curve, and he
didn't see her, so he plowed into her.
(calls off)
Do you remember Daddy and I came through the back door,
Mama? And Nancy was hanging out of his arms like a set of
broken-up bagpipes. And he spread her out on the kitchen
floor and she was breathing real hard. And the pain was hum-
ming off of her like I could hear it. And she just let the pain
take her over. And that's all she was. This *pained* thing.

*(Gertie enters with a cookie tin. CLAIRE's story has
brought her back into the room.)*

CLAIRE

And Daddy was bent over her, talking to her real quiet. And all of a sudden Nancy stood up, like it was a new day, and she started running around the kitchen like she wasn't half-dead, barking and clicking her nails against the floor tiles. And we were all shocked because Nancy was like a puppy all of a sudden, not that bony heap on the floor. She was this fire-ball for about three minutes, until she got tired again, and curled up beside the sink and went to sleep and died like it meant nothing. You remember how all that happened in here? It's funny how almost everything else is gone to me, and that sad old dog just came into my head.

GERTIE

(hands her tin)
Clay . . .

CLAIRE

Cookies? You're tearin' this place apart for cookies?

GERTIE

Pen-o, Clay. Toe-phoes.

(GERTIE looks to the basement, worried. CLAIRE opens the tin and pulls out some old photos.)

CLAIRE

Ooo, pictures.
(picks up photo)
Is this me? This little girl is me, isn't it? Oh what a cutie I was.

GERTIE

Cutie Clay.

CLAIRE

(another photo)
That's you and . . . Daddy?

GERTIE

(nods)
Mm-hmm.

CLAIRE

In front of the tree that Zack climbed. Happy-happy-people.
(another photo)
Oh, what . . . what's this? It's all weird.

GERTIE

Za.

CLAIRE

Zack?

GERTIE

Ada fay. Ih da fuhnus. Da meers.

CLAIRE

Meers?

GERTIE

Ih da fuhnus. Fuddy meers.
(holds up reflective tin cover)
Meers.

CLAIRE

Mirrors?

GERTIE

Ih Piehmoe.

CLAIRE

Piermont? The Piermont Fair?

GERTIE

Da Piehmoe fay!

CLAIRE

We went every spring.

GERTIE

An da Za in da fuddy meers.

CLAIRE

The funhouse mirrors.

GERTIE

Yada tooda pitue oh Za ih da fuddy meers.

CLAIRE

This is Zack? He looks all warped and twisted up. This isn't
Zack.

GERTIE

Edadly!

CLAIRE

I don't understand.

GERTIE

Da ih Za, Clay. He feh oh da tee.

CLAIRE

In the funhouse, but this isn't—

GERTIE

You doe mem ohta tins dah happy.

(*The echoey carnival music pipes in.* CLAIRE *taps
her head with the palm of her hand.*)

CLAIRE

Oops. Here we go again. Music time.

GERTIE

Clay?

CLAIRE

It'll pass in a second. Although . . .
(*struggles with a memory*)
I'm seeing a frying pan. Should that ring any bells?

GERTIE

Yesh! Da fyin pay!

(We hear the men approaching.)

LIMPING MAN
(off)
Letth load theethe thleeping bagth into the back of the car.

MILLET
(off, as puppet)
I bet they're musty and crawling with bugs!

GERTIE
Dogdambit!

(GERTIE gathers up photos and pushes tin aside. The music stops.)

CLAIRE
There. It's gone again.

(MILLET and Limping Man enter, cuffless.)

LIMPING MAN
You were good, right Gertie? Played by the roolth? Like we thaid?

GERTIE
Cursive. Ida nevoo crotch you.

LIMPING MAN
Good. You've been a firth-clath hothteth. But our party ith moving on.

MILLET
(puppet)
No more manacles, see?

CLAIRE
Where you going, Zack?

LIMPING MAN
Jutht for a drive. Grab your thtuff. Letth go!

MILLET

I didn't know she was coming with us.

CLAIRE

I wanna stay with Mama.

LIMPING MAN

Claire, we need to get you thomewhere thafe. You don't think that huthband of yourth ithn't gonna figure thith out? You don't think he'th gonna make hith way to Gertie'th houthe?

CLAIRE

I don't really know him that well.

LIMPING MAN

Egthactly. Thath why you need to rely on me. He'll find you. Won't he, Gertie? Tell Claire here that she needth to leave with me and Millet.

MILLET

That wasn't the plan. I thought you just wanted to talk to her.

LIMPING MAN

Go warm up the car.

MILLET
    (as puppet)
He's not warming up nothing, gimpy!

LIMPING MAN

Binky—

CLAIRE

I don't want to go for a drive.

MILLET
    (as puppet)
She doesn't wanna go for a drive.

LIMPING MAN

Millet—

MILLET

Binky—

GERTIE

Clay—

LIMPING MAN

Gertie, explain to her how she hath to go with uth.

GERTIE

Noda Za, Clay. Ee feh oh da tee.

LIMPING MAN

Gertie'th had a thtroke. She geth all muddled thometimth. Right, Gertie?

GERTIE
(to LIMPING MAN*)*
Yuca keelush, Fee, buhda woe cha-cha nuddy!

LIMPING MAN

Thtroke victimth are eathily upthet. She'th like thith all the time.

MILLET
(as puppet)
Lies, Millet! All lies!

LIMPING MAN
(to MILLET*)*
Get the mapth out of the glove compartment—

MILLET

That wasn't the plan!

LIMPING MAN

And review the route.

(GERTIE *has opened tin and pulled out old news-*
paper article.)

GERTIE
(pushing article at CLAIRE)
Ree, Clay! Ree!

MILLET
(puppet to LIMPING MAN)
You're not in charge of him!

CLAIRE
(looking at article)
What is this?

MILLET
(puppet to LIMPING MAN)
You're not his mother!

GERTIE
Ih tess wha happy!

LIMPING MAN
What'd you give her, Gertie?!

CLAIRE
It's Zack's obituary.

LIMPING MAN
She'th crazy, Claire. Ever thince the thtroke.

CLAIRE
It says Zack died when he was eight.

(LIMPING MAN *grabs obituary from* CLAIRE.)

MILLET
We had *meetings* about the plan.

GERTIE

He feh oh da tee!

CLAIRE

He fell out of the tree!

MILLET

And now everything changes all of a sudden.

LIMPING MAN

(to MILLET*)*
Get in the fucking car!

CLAIRE

He climbed too high and fell.

LIMPING MAN

Thath a different boy, Claire!

CLAIRE

Zack died.

(KENNY, HEIDI, *and* RICHARD, *holding up bacon, appear in the window.)*

RICHARD

Somebody lose some bacon?

(Everyone screams.)

RICHARD

What the devil's going on here?

CLAIRE

(to RICHARD*)*
Stay away! They told me everything!

RICHARD

I'm coming around the front!

(RICHARD, KENNY, *and* HEIDI *exit window.)*

CLAIRE

Oh no, he's coming around the front!

(GERTIE *grabs kitchen knife and raises it.*)

LIMPING MAN

Claire, quick, out the window!

GERTIE

Egg dis!

(GERTIE *stabs* LIMPING MAN *in the back. He screams and falls to the ground in pain.*)

MILLET

What's happening?!

LIMPING MAN

The old crone thtabbed me!

MILLET

Aw geez!

LIMPING MAN

Don't you leave me, Millet!

MILLET

This is bad. This is very bad.

(GERTIE *rushes to phone and dials 911.*)

CLAIRE

Mama, I gotta hide from Richard Fiffle!

MILLET

This is what happens when we change the plan.

GERTIE
(into phone)
Isis Geht Maso! *Fee cape!* I dabbed him inda bag!

(MILLET *is about to run out when* RICHARD *runs in, followed by* KENNY, *who leads* HEIDI *in at gunpoint.*)

MILLET

It's the cops!
(*tries to hide*)

KENNY

What the hell?!

RICHARD

(*to* HEIDI)
Look! What did I tell you? Claire!

CLAIRE

(*to* RICHARD)
Stay away from me!

GERTIE

(*into phone*)
Ona four ohda clickin!
(*sees* HEIDI)
Oh, dear heah.

LIMPING MAN

Millet, call a doctor!

MILLET

Okay, call a doctor.

KENNY

Are you okay, Mom?

CLAIRE

Gertie stabbed the deformed man!

MILLET

(*to* GERTIE)
Gimme the phone!

GERTIE

No! Iss my-pho! Fug-dew!

RICHARD

Claire—

CLAIRE

(runs away)
Help!

RICHARD

Would someone tell her I'm the nice guy?!

HEIDI

(going to LIMPING MAN*)*
Who did this to you?!

LIMPING MAN

(points to GERTIE*)*
She did! She did it!

HEIDI

(to KENNY*)*
All right, gimme my gun.

KENNY

No way, that's my grandmother.

> *(In the confusion,* HEIDI *tries to wrestle the gun from* KENNY's *hand. They struggle while* LIMPING MAN *writhes on the ground.* MILLET *tries to get phone from* GERTIE. RICHARD *pursues* CLAIRE.)*

RICHARD

But Claire, we've been looking for you.

CLAIRE

I heard about the paperweight!

HEIDI
(struggling with KENNY*)*
Let go of the gun, pot-head!

LIMPING MAN
(referring to GERTIE*)*
Knock her out, Millet!

MILLET
(as puppet, struggling with GERTIE*)*
Don't tell him what to do!

KENNY
You're gonna shoot the wrong people!

GERTIE
Ah! My pho!

MILLET
(as puppet)
My-pho! My-pho!

RICHARD
You were safe with me, Claire.

CLAIRE
Get him away!

LIMPING MAN
You thcrewed me, Gertie! You shouldn't have done that!

*(*GERTIE *snatches the puppet and raises the knife.)*

GERTIE
Dab da fuddin puppa!
(stabs the puppet repeatedly)

MILLET
Ah! Hinky Binky!
(as puppet)
Help! She's killing me!

HEIDI
(all overlapping)
It's *my* gun! You
drugged-out little
twirp!

LIMPING MAN
(all overlapping)
I'm bleeding to death!
Stupid old lady! Look
what you did!

MILLET
(all overlapping)
She's killing me! Oh, the
pain is unbearable!

KENNY
(all overlapping)
Let go of it! You don't
know who anybody is!

RICHARD
(all overlapping)
It's okay, Claire. Don't
believe anything this
man has told you.

GERTIE
(all overlapping)
Kee da puppa! Doopy
fuddin puppa! Die! Die!

*(A cacophony of noise from all of them. GERTIE stab-
bing HINKY BINKY. KENNY wrestling with HEIDI.
RICHARD pursuing CLAIRE. MILLET screaming as
the puppet. LIMPING MAN in agony. Then CLAIRE
lets out a long wail.)*

CLAIRE
Stoooooooooooooooooooooppppp iiiiiiiiiiiiiiit!

(The gun goes off. Blackout.)

Act Two

Scene One

(In darkness we hear the gunshot. Lights up on
GERTIE's *kitchen, where we left off.* CLAIRE *seems to*
be a little out of it. KENNY *has been shot in the arm.)*

KENNY

Aawwwww, God.
(holds his arm in pain)

RICHARD

Are you okay, Kenny?

KENNY

I've been shot!

LIMPING MAN

I've been thtabbed!

MILLET

My Binky got cut!

GERTIE

An noon onion stammy!

HEIDI

(stands with gun)
Anyone moves, I'll shoot you a new asshole!

RICHARD
(to HEIDI*)*
Now you see why I was in a hurry? Check my wife. She has
amnesia.

HEIDI
Don't tell me what to do!

GERTIE
(points frantically at LIMPING MAN*)*
Ish axel is genderlish!

HEIDI
What?!

GERTIE
Ee hersh poopoos!

RICHARD
She's absolutely right.

HEIDI
Millet—

MILLET
Yes?

HEIDI
Get the knife.

MILLET
But Hinky Binky got hurt and—

HEIDI
Just get the knife.

(Everyone's confused. MILLET *takes knife from* GERTIE.*)*

GERTIE
I doan onion stammish.

MILLET

Here's the knife.

HEIDI

Good. Now if anyone moves, stab them in the head.
(indicates RICHARD*)*
And watch this bozo. He knows how to disarm people.
(goes to LIMPING MAN*)*
How you doing, baby? Got stabbed, huh?

LIMPING MAN

You were thuppothed to watch them. You were thuppothed to detain them and make sure they didn't get up here.

HEIDI

Well, it didn't go as planned.

KENNY

(realizing)
Oh, man . . .

RICHARD

Do you all know each other?

LIMPING MAN

Did you get the pathportth?

HEIDI

Yeah, Twitchy hooked me up with a guy in Bingham.

CLAIRE

Would someone tell me what's going on?
(beat)
Would someone tell me one bit of truthful information . . .
please?

> *(Silence. They all look around at each other. After a couple beats,* GERTIE *finally steps forward to clear things up.)*

GERTIE

Ida gnome mower, Clay. Evatin row when Za feh oda tee. Da die. Oomay Fee an bah tin happy. Deh oo fie bah an deh figit. An I hada toke, so king talk bah. Fee heah an evatin bah gin. Evatin bah gin, Clay.

CLAIRE
                    (beat)
What the fuck are you talking about?!!!

RICHARD
Claire . . .

CLAIRE
                    (banging palms against her head)
I'm sorry. I'm not myself today.

RICHARD
Don't whack your head, honey.

HEIDI
                    (comforting LIMPING MAN*)*
Aww, look at Mister Bloody.

KENNY
Oh, I'm sorry, did I mention I've been shot? Well I *was*!

LIMPING MAN
Claire wath a nurth. She can help uth.

CLAIRE
                    (stops banging head)
What?

HEIDI
Millet, take the husband and the old lady to the basement.

MILLET
But my free-basing mom used to lock me in the basement!

CLAIRE

I was a nurse?

MILLET

We have to go back to the plan!

LIMPING MAN

All right, we'll go back to the plan!

CLAIRE

Did I wear nurse's shoes?

KENNY

I'll tell you what happened, Mom.

RICHARD AND LIMPING MAN

Kenny, no!

(RICHARD *and* LIMPING MAN *look at each other.*)

RICHARD

Remember what the doctors said, Kenny. There were strict instructions.

LIMPING MAN

Better lithen to your Dad.

(KENNY *turns his attention to his wound.*)

HEIDI

Get them out of here, Millet.

MILLET

I have to lock ya in the basement.

RICHARD
(*to* CLAIRE)

Nothing to worry about, Claire. Everything's gonna be Jim Dandy!

MILLET

Keep moving!
    (leads GERTIE *and* RICHARD *to the basement)*

KENNY

Hello! Bullet wound on the child! Am I *invisible*?!

HEIDI

You were *grazed*.

KENNY

I'm still *bleeding*, bitch.

HEIDI
    (to CLAIRE*)*
You're raising a misogynist. You're a terrible mother.

CLAIRE

I am? Oh dear. I thought I might be.

LIMPING MAN

Look at all the carnage. Remindth me of when I wath in
Nam.

KENNY

You were never in Nam.

CLAIRE

Okay, maybe we need supplies. Nurse's supplies. Let's see,
what do I need?
    (beat)
I guess I don't know what we need.

HEIDI

She's useless.

KENNY

She has amnesia, dumb-ass.

HEIDI
(hands gun to LIMPING MAN*)*
Take the gun. I'm gonna check the medicine cabinet. If they
try anything, shoot them in the head.
(exits)

CLAIRE
She seems to have a bit of a chip on her shoulder.
(turns to KENNY*)*
Hey, what kind of nurse was I anyway?

KENNY
A school nurse.

CLAIRE
Oh, I bet my uniform was very starched.

LIMPING MAN
(grabs nearby towel)
Take thith, Kenny. Hold it tight to thtop thome of the bleeding.

KENNY
Fuck you.

LIMPING MAN
You're an angry little man. Thath a terrible thing to be.

(CLAIRE *takes towel and brings it to* KENNY's *arm.*)

CLAIRE
Yes, apply pressure, stop the bleeding. This is familiar. All
those kids running in from the playground with scrapes and
cuts and cigarette burns and souvenir paperweights sticking
out of their foreheads.
(beat)
Is that right? That doesn't seem right to me.

LIMPING MAN
Hey, Claire?

CLAIRE
Yeah, Zack?

KENNY

His name is Philip.

CLAIRE

Right. He's *Philip* pretending to be Zack, who fell out of the tree. Sorry. It's so hard to keep it all straight.

LIMPING MAN

Look at my back. Can you thtitch it up?

CLAIRE
          (examines his back)
Oh sure. I've seen much worse than that. God knows I don't know *where.*
          (moves to KENNY*)*
No stitches for you, Kenny. Just a nice clean bandage.
          (pause as she looks at him)
I wasn't really a bad mother, was I? What the lady just said, is it true?

KENNY

No. She doesn't know you. You were a good mother.

CLAIRE

Oh good.
          (remembers)
Six pounds, fourteen ounces.
          (beat)
That's how much you weighed at birth.

KENNY
          (wants to tell her)
Mom . . .

CLAIRE

Yes?

KENNY
          (looks over at LIMPING MAN*)*
Never mind.

          *(Lights out on them. The echoey dog barking tran-
          sitions us into—)*

Scene Two

(Lights up in the basement. MILLET *stands guard over* RICHARD *and* GERTIE.*)*

MILLET

Nobody better try anything 'cause I've been tricked too many times today.

GERTIE

Dash biggo yoo-zo doopy.

MILLET

Don't talk jibberish. I'm sure you just said something very mean about me.
(as puppet)
So . . . much . . . pain . . .
(normal)
And look what you did to Hinky Binky.
(puppet)
Everything's going dark.
(normal)
Hang in there, Bink.
(puppet)
Millet, is that you?
(normal)
I'm here. Be brave little puppet.

RICHARD

Damn. You're crazy.

MILLET

You got a sewing kit in this dungeon?

GERTIE

Yah. Maybe ova nose bachus.

MILLET

Well, go get it. I gotta fix my friend.

GERTIE

Uh . . . Oday. Aybee ride bag.

(GERTIE *goes off into other part of the basement.*)

MILLET

I'm watching you, old lady, so don't get funny.

GERTIE

(off)

Nuddin fuddy heah.

RICHARD

Look, I don't know what you people have in mind, but it's not worth wrecking your life. Believe me, I know.

MILLET

I'm not talking to you. Talk gets me in trouble. My lip is zipped, Sporto.

RICHARD

I know where your head is right now. You're probably strung out, doin' whatever you can to scrounge up the next fix.

MILLET

What?

RICHARD

Sure, I look like an upright guy, nice family, good job at the hospital, but I've been right where you're standing, buddy-boy.

MILLET

(calls off)

Gertie, my Binky is dying!

GERTIE

(off)

Ahm dill loodin!

RICHARD

She said she's still looking.

MILLET

I know what she said.

GERTIE
(crosses with a photo album)
I tink iss up in da clickin.
(exits upstairs)

MILLET

Hey! She's a slippery one, isn't she?

RICHARD

You gotta open your eyes, my friend. You are mixed up with a
very bad crowd.

MILLET
(weak puppet)
I can't feel my toes.

RICHARD

I was in deep, just like you. And *I* got out.

MILLET
(weak puppet)
Are you a doctor?

RICHARD
(beat)
No. I work at the hospital, but I'm just a technician. I run the
MRIs. That's how I met Claire.

MILLET
(weak puppet)
So, you can't help me . . . MRI guy?

RICHARD

I'm sorry, puppet. I can't.

MILLET
(normal)
We'll stitch you up in no time, Binky.

RICHARD
This is crazy— This is— This is—
(loses it)
There is a woman upstairs with a *medical* condition! She is
probably very disoriented and frightened and in physical danger, and if that guy—!!!

MILLET
Stop yelling at me! Why are you yelling at me?!

RICHARD
I'm sorry. I just . . . I should never have taken that shower.

GERTIE
(off)
I gut da doe-in-tit.

RICHARD
Someday, if you're very lucky, you're gonna get everything you
ever wanted in life. And when someone tries to take it away,
then you'll understand why I was yelling.

(GERTIE *comes back carrying a sewing kit and a
photo album.*)

GERTIE
Heah da doe-in-tit.
(hands sewing kit to MILLET*)*

MILLET
I'm gonna stay over here and sew up Binky. Nobody come
near me. I've got a knife.

RICHARD
You're not gonna use it.

MILLET

Oh shut up.

GERTIE

Loo ah dese toe-phos, Record.

   (She brings album to RICHARD. *They flip through it.)*

RICHARD

I'm not really in the mood to look at photos, Gert.

GERTIE

Loo ah dis one dough. Is da weddin dah.

RICHARD

Gosh, look at that. Claire in a wedding dress. So young.
   (spots another photo)
And is that Phil doing the chicken dance?

GERTIE

Sumna-bitch.

RICHARD

Weird. He looks normal. Nice ears. Both sides working.

GERTIE

Mean sumnabitch.

RICHARD

   (another photo)
And there's you with the bouquet. You look mad.

GERTIE

I coo tah den. Bach den evabiddy onion stammy. I wizz-eye
hat . . .
   (tries very hard to say this)
Iiii wiissh . . . I had . . . sehd sssummttiiinnn weeeehnn . . . I
c-could.

RICHARD
(pause)
You know what I wish? I wish I never did drugs, or robbed
houses, or resisted arrest, but I did all those things. And the
best I can do is make up for it.

MILLET
I stole some toilet paper from the janitor's closet once. I felt
terrible about that, but I was all out at home.

RICHARD
(new photo)
That's a nice photo of you, Gert. Digging out in the garden . . .
Digging with your *shovel*.

GERTIE
Digga widda shova.

MILLET
(still sewing)
Digga widda shova.

GERTIE
Aybee rye bag.
(runs off into other part of basement)

MILLET
Come back here! I'm guarding you!

GERTIE
(off)
Toe-phoes! Thall! Toe-phoes!

MILLET
I'm a terrible guard.

RICHARD
What's your name anyway?

MILLET

Millet.
(reconsiders suddenly)
I mean Hector.

RICHARD

Don't you wanna change, Millet?

MILLET

My name is Hector, I said!

RICHARD

Isn't there something you've always wanted to do? Be a
teacher? A lawyer?

MILLET
(puppet)
Zoo keeper. He always wanted to be a zoo keeper.
(normal, happy to see the puppet has recovered)
Binky!

RICHARD

Well there you go. You can do that. It's not too late to be a zoo
keeper. And the first step is helping us, because you know it's
right.

MILLET

Phil is here to make up with her. I *am* doing right.

RICHARD

You don't believe that. You know he's lied to you like he's lied
to everyone.

MILLET

I'm not listening!

(GERTIE, *rummaging, knocks something over.*)

GERTIE
(off)
Dem pick gog shit! Fuddin' shit!

RICHARD

This hostage stuff isn't the life you want. Kidnapping an inno-
cent woman, lying to her, getting her family upset . . .

MILLET

(puppet adds to list)
Bringing her to Canada.

RICHARD

Canada?

MILLET

Binky!

RICHARD

He's bringing Claire to Canada?

MILLET

(to RICHARD*)*
Don't talk to us! I hate this basement! It's like truth serum!

RICHARD

Claire doesn't wanna go to Canada, and you know that. You
can end it here. You just stop and say, "I've had enough. Today
I'm a good person." That's what I did. And it worked.

MILLET

How?

RICHARD

I'll tell you how. Polly Harkness.

MILLET

Gertie?!

GERTIE

(off)
I'm loodin!

RICHARD

I loved that woman more than life. She worked at the hard-
ware store. And I wanted to marry her, but I didn't have any
money to get a ring, so I got stoned and decided to find a lady
with the same size fingers and rob her. Take *her* wedding ring.

MILLET
(something bothers him)
You were gonna steal somebody's ring?

RICHARD

I was a bad man. Now you see how we're the same?

GERTIE
(off)
I ding I fow da bach, Record!

RICHARD

I searched all day and finally spotted a lady with the same size
and build coming out of a school, getting into her car. She
never saw me. I knocked her over the head with a rock, and
she was out. And I took her ring.

MILLET
(still trying to figure it out)
With a nice diamond in the middle, and two rubies on the
side?

RICHARD

Right. I offered it to Polly on my knees, and she said no. Because there was blood on it. And she'd never marry a know-
nothin druggie. So I decided to change, mostly to spite her. I
went back to school and learned how to run the MRI ma-
chines, and that's how I met Claire. And guess who's wearing
that ring right now?

GERTIE
(off)
Damma fuddin shova!

RICHARD
Now do you see what you can accomplish?

MILLET
I knew that ring looked familiar. I'm so stupid!

RICHARD
You okay, Gertie?!

MILLET
You can't hurt people like that and have someone else take the blame!

GERTIE
(off)
I guddit!

MILLET
(stalking Richard)
You can't hurt people like that.

RICHARD
I don't anymore. That's my point.

MILLET
You should never hurt people. Never.

> (MILLET *chases* RICHARD *into the darkness of the basement offstage. From a different part of the basement,* GERTIE *comes running out of the darkness with a raised shovel. She runs after an oblivious* MILLET. *Offstage we hear the metalic thwack of a shovel hitting his head. Lights out.*
>
> *A strange jumbled overlapping of carnival music, dog barking, 70's easy-listening, and radio scanning transitions us into—)*

Scene Three

(Lights up in the kitchen. CLAIRE *is bandaging* KENNY's *arm.* LIMPING MAN *tries to thread a needle.* HEIDI *is pacing.)*

HEIDI
Jesus! This is taking too long.
(to CLAIRE)
Stitch up his back.

CLAIRE
(still with KENNY)
Almost done.

HEIDI
You said we'd be in and out. You said "a few words."

LIMPING MAN
And you thaid you'd watch the huthband!

HEIDI
This is screwy. Some big apology to someone who isn't even gonna remember it.

LIMPING MAN
I'll remember it.

CLAIRE
Ooo, there's an apology coming?

HEIDI
We don't have a lot of time, Phil.

CLAIRE
Excuse me, did you help him break out of jail?

HEIDI

Yes I did. We're in love.

CLAIRE

Gosh, a convict and a lady cop.

HEIDI

I'm not really a lady cop. I just stole the uniform from the
laundry truck.

LIMPING MAN

What are you doing?

HEIDI

It's not like she's gonna remember.
    (to CLAIRE)
I'm really a kitchen worker. I prepare the prison meals.

KENNY

You're a lunch lady?

HEIDI

I do dinners too!

CLAIRE

And you met in the kitchen?

HEIDI

Yeah. Phil was on dish duty. He caught my eye while scraping
plates.

CLAIRE

How sweet. And now you're on the lam. You must really love
each other.

HEIDI

I just said we did.

CLAIRE

Did you? Oh, I must've forgot. Did Philip say it too? Because
I don't remember him mentioning it.

LIMPING MAN
You almotht done there, Claire?

HEIDI
Hey, he loves me, okay? We're going to Canada together. Tell her how we're going to Canada.

LIMPING MAN
We're going to Canada.

HEIDI
I'm gonna tell you something, lady. I went out on a limb for this man. I laced the guards pulled-pork sandwiches. Have you ever done anything like that for him?

CLAIRE
I don't know.

HEIDI
I love him, you understand? And he loves me. Don't you, Phil?
     (pause)
Phil?

CLAIRE
He's deaf in that ear. Maybe he didn't hear you.

HEIDI
Don't you love me, Phil?!

LIMPING MAN
     (pause)
Of courth I do.

HEIDI
     (turns to CLAIRE*)*
See? I told you.

CLAIRE
Can you get me some ice from the freezer?

     *(*HEIDI *goes to the freezer.)*

CLAIRE
(to LIMPING MAN*)*
You got yourself a fire-cracker there.
(to KENNY*)*
All done.

KENNY
Thanks.

CLAIRE
(to LIMPING MAN*)*
Your turn.

(GERTIE *enters from the basment, carrying a photo album.)*

GERTIE
Heddo, dis geddin da doe-in-tit.

(GERTIE *grabs the sewing kit, leaving behind a few needles and spools of thread.)*

GERTIE
(calls down into basement)
I gut da doe-in-tit.
(exits into basment)

LIMPING MAN
(referring to MILLET*)*
He's a terrible guard.

(HEIDI *comes back with frozen-food items.* CLAIRE *cleans* PHIL'S *wound.)*

HEIDI
No ice. Just frozen food. Ground beef, Tater-Tots, a pound of bacon—

LIMPING MAN
No bacon! Put the bacon back! You should know! What did I thay about bacon?!

HEIDI
(pause)
I'm sorry. I'll put the bacon back.
(She does.)

(CLAIRE holds frozen food to PHILIP's back. He winces.)

CLAIRE
It's very odd.

LIMPING MAN
What?

CLAIRE
This whole bacon thing.

LIMPING MAN
I don't wanna talk about it.

CLAIRE
Are you a vegetarian?

LIMPING MAN
Am I what?

HEIDI
He's just mad because I blabbed.

LIMPING MAN
Well Jethuth, Heidi, the whole plan hinged on abtholute the-
crethy!

HEIDI
She has *amnesia*!

LIMPING MAN
The *boy* has ears!

KENNY
Yeah, nice ones too. Not like my Dad's.

LIMPING MAN

Kenny—

CLAIRE

What's he talking about?

LIMPING MAN

Nothing. Your kidth a little thlow. He thez weird thingth all
the time.

KENNY

This guy's my father.

LIMPING MAN

Goddamit, Kenny.

CLAIRE

What?

KENNY

You were married to him for 19 years.

CLAIRE

I thought Richard Fiffle was my husband.

KENNY

Second husband.

LIMPING MAN

I wath waiting for the right time to tell you.

HEIDI

He's really sorry.
        (*to* LIMPING MAN)
Can we go now?

CLAIRE

Sorry for what?

KENNY

Dad's got a short fuse, and a killer left hook.

LIMPING MAN

Kenny, you are breaking the roolth!
(*turns to* CLAIRE)
Look, I wath gonna tell you everything. But then they all popped up in the window, and the puppet thcreamed, and Gertie thtuck a knife in my back.

CLAIRE

Why were you in jail?

KENNY

He set our house on fire.

LIMPING MAN

I wath provoked!

CLAIRE

You burned our house down?

LIMPING MAN

I yoothed to have a temper, but I'm thweeter than cuthtard now. Athk Heidi.

HEIDI

Just put in the stitches so we can go.

LIMPING MAN

I've had a lot of countheling, Claire.

KENNY

Sounds like you've made great strides.

HEIDI

Shoot him! *Shoot* him!

LIMPING MAN

Heidi, I'm not gonna shoot my own kid.

(beat)
A couple yearth ago, I might've, but not anymore.

HEIDI

Gimme that fucking needle, I'll do it myself.
(grabs sewing supplies)

LIMPING MAN

Heidi, you don't know how to—

HEIDI

I took Home Ec!
(gets to work on sewing his wound)

KENNY

Tell her the rest!

LIMPING MAN

Kenny, you don't know how good I was in prithon.

CLAIRE

(more to herself)
Richard Fiffle didn't beat me.

LIMPING MAN

(stuck by needle)
Ow!

HEIDI

Sorry.

CLAIRE

Zack and I were playing. And he fell.

LIMPING MAN

I worked hard, Claire. And rehabilitated mythelf.

HEIDI

Hold still.

LIMPING MAN
I did crafth. Made dioramath out of popthicle thtickth.

CLAIRE
You lied when you took me away.

LIMPING MAN
I read the Bible.

HEIDI
He wrote me poems.

CLAIRE
You wrote her poems?

LIMPING MAN
(to CLAIRE)
You were the inthpiration.
(stuck by needle)
Ow!

HEIDI
No she wasn't.

LIMPING MAN
(in pain)
Jethuth, Heidi.

CLAIRE
(sorting it out)
And Nancy died here.

HEIDI
Those poems were mine, Phil.
(to CLAIRE)
He wrote one called "Heidi's Hairnet."
(to PHIL)
It wasn't called "Claire's Hairnet."

KENNY

Tell her the rest. Before jail.

LIMPING MAN

Kenny—
          (stuck)
Heidi!

KENNY

Do you remember my birthday, Mom?

CLAIRE

May third.

KENNY

May third. She's coming back strong. Do you remember the day I turned fifteen?

CLAIRE

No.

KENNY

It was almost two years ago, the day your brain zorched.

LIMPING MAN

Come on, she doethn't—

KENNY

You said you were gonna tell her everything.

CLAIRE

You did say that, Phil.

LIMPING MAN

Yeah but I—ow!

CLAIRE

Fifteenth birthday. Go on.

KENNY

The plan was, you were gonna take me to the Piermont Fair.

CLAIRE

That's where my Dad took me and Zack.

KENNY

Exactly what you said. Sounded like fun. And Phil didn't wanna go.

LIMPING MAN

I don't like fairth.

KENNY

Which was fine by me.

LIMPING MAN

Carnieth give me the creepth.

KENNY

So that morning, we got up early. You set out the Fruity Pebbles and we were about to leave. Only he woke up and said he didn't want no Fruity Pebbles, he wanted a *hot* breakfast.

LIMPING MAN

I wathn't feeling good, Claire. I needed thomething thubthtantial in my thtomach.

KENNY

But we were about to go, so I asked him why he couldn't make his own breakfast, which I guess was out of line.

LIMPING MAN

Look, whath important ith I've changed.

KENNY

Because he leaned back, made a fist and clocked me.

LIMPING MAN

That wath the only time I hit that kid. Tell her that.

KENNY

He's right. He knocked you against the wall every day of the week, but that was the only time he hit me.

LIMPING MAN

I did not hit you every day. He exaggerayth.

HEIDI

I said don't move.

KENNY

So I'm sitting there, cartoon birdies flying around my head—

LIMPING MAN

He'th not remembering it right.

KENNY

And he starts throwing things around the kitchen.

LIMPING MAN

Nothing breakable.

KENNY

Things broke.

LIMPING MAN

Thith kid'th not right in the head, Claire.

KENNY

And he's over me screaming that fifteen is too old to go to a fair. That it must be a fairy fair.

LIMPING MAN

You won't remember thith, but I dropped him ath a baby. All the time.

KENNY

And you're just standing at the stove.

LIMPING MAN

I wath a total butterfingerth.

KENNY

Making him the eggs and bacon he asked for.

LIMPING MAN

Tho hith head ith a little off.

HEIDI

Also he's stoned.

KENNY

I remember this!

LIMPING MAN

Claire, I'm here to apologithe. I wish none of that happened. Thath why I'm here.

KENNY

Hold on, we're getting to the good part.

LIMPING MAN

Ow!

KENNY

You're frying up the bacon, nice and crisp the way he likes it, and he says—

LIMPING MAN

I'm not a unique perthon.

KENNY

And he says, "Never mind, I'm not hungry anymore."

LIMPING MAN

Many men hit people. And a lot of them learn how to thtop.

KENNY

And he goes into the bedroom and slams the door.

CLAIRE

And he falls back to sleep.

KENNY

(beat)
That's *right*. Because a good tantrum always knocked him out.

CLAIRE

And I tell you to go wait in the car—

LIMPING MAN

Claire—

CLAIRE

—because we were going to Piermont.

KENNY

So I limp to the car.

CLAIRE

And I pick up the frying pan and walk into the bedroom, and he's sleeping on his side. And I drain the scalding bacon grease into his ear.

KENNY

And I hear the scream through the bedroom door, and the storm door and the screen door and the car door. All those doors, but I can still hear that scream.

CLAIRE

And I come outside and throw the frying pan into the bushes and get in the car. And we drive to Piermont in silence.
(pause)
And then what happened?

KENNY

We rode on the ferris wheel

CLAIRE

Uh-huh.

KENNY

And the tilt-a-whirl

CLAIRE

Right.

KENNY

And we went to the fun house.

CLAIRE

And in the funhouse were the funny mirrors that made everything all warped and stretched.

KENNY

And you said your brother Zack loved that best.

CLAIRE

He did.

KENNY

And you said the two of you would dance in the funny mirrors and your Dad would take pictures of the twisted reflections.

CLAIRE

I said that?

KENNY

Yeah.

CLAIRE

And then what happened?

KENNY

You fainted. And when you woke up, everything was gone. You didn't remember anything. It was all gone.

(silence)

LIMPING MAN

Well whoopty-doo. There you have it, all wrapped in a big red
bow.
(to KENNY)
You done, kid?

CLAIRE

You shouldn't be so flip.

LIMPING MAN

But Claire, the whole point ith I'm not that perthon anymore.

HEIDI

(breaks thread)
You're done. Let's go.

LIMPING MAN

Look, I'm thorry I thet the houthe on fire while you were at
the fair. I wath mad. But now . . . Now I'm glad you poured
that bacon greathe in my ear. You know why? Becauthe it
burned the bad part out of me. The bad bit ith a dead bulb.
Only the good parth twinkle now.

KENNY

(to LIMPING MAN)
You can leave.

LIMPING MAN

We're gonna go to Canada. Millet hath a friend who'll hide uth.
(beat)
Come with uth, Claire.

HEIDI

Phil—

LIMPING MAN

Whath one more perthon?

HEIDI

This wasn't the plan.

LIMPING MAN

Planth change.

HEIDI

You said *talk* to her, not *bring* her.

LIMPING MAN

Claire, we can thtart over.

HEIDI

You motherfucker.

LIMPING MAN

Heidi, you gotta underthtand.

HEIDI

Suck my ass, Phil.

LIMPING MAN

Juth go get Millet. We'll all talk about it.

HEIDI

Yeah, I'll go get Millet, and then he and I will leave here without you.

LIMPING MAN

Heidi—
    (reaches out to her)

HEIDI

Don't touch me! I am not her! I'll kick the shit of you, you deformed monkey!
    (calls off)
Millet?!
    (exits into basement)

LIMPING MAN

    (beat)
Thath okay. We can take my car.
    *(*CLAIRE *doesn't move.)*

LIMPING MAN

Come on, Claire. It wathn't all like he thaid.

(to KENNY)

Tell her about the Monopoly gaymth. And the thurch-a-wordth.

(to CLAIRE)

We would do thurch-a-word puthelth together. You and me, on the couch. And I'd braid your hair. Remember how I'd braid your hair?

(no response)

I love you, Claire. We've shared a life. For better or worth, it wath ourth. And I love you. Now leth go.

(KENNY *makes a mad scramble for the gun.* LIMP-ING MAN *is confused.* KENNY *suddenly has the gun pointed at* LIMPING MAN.)

KENNY

She doesn't want to go.

LIMPING MAN

What are you doing?

CLAIRE

Don't play with guns, honey.

KENNY

She's not going with you.

LIMPING MAN

I know you're mad, kiddo. I'm thorry for what I did. I don't know how elthe to thay it to you.

CLAIRE

Put the gun down, Kenny.

LIMPING MAN

You know, there wath a time when you couldn't tie your shooth. Do you remember?

KENNY

She's not going.

LIMPING MAN

And then I taught you. You remember that thummer at the lake? And now you know how to tie your shooth, right?

KENNY

Just say you're leaving without her.

LIMPING MAN

People can learn thingth, Kenny. People can change.

CLAIRE

Please sweetie, give it to me.

> (*Pause.* KENNY *reluctantly hands the gun to her. She throws it out the window.*)

LIMPING MAN

Uh, I kinda needed that.

CLAIRE

What'd you do to us?

LIMPING MAN

I wish you remembered thome of the good thingth.

CLAIRE

So do I.

LIMPING MAN

Becauthe, there were . . . thome good thingth.

CLAIRE

Yeah, that lake thing you just said sounded nice.

LIMPING MAN

It wath. And we can go back there. Rent the cottage, get thome inner-toobth, bug thpray—

(CLAIRE *seems to have a flash of pain across her head. We hear puppies yapping.*)

KENNY

Mom?

CLAIRE

I'm okay. I just . . . I think I've got one.

KENNY

One what?

CLAIRE
(*to* LIMPING MAN)
The first time we met. That's a good one, right?

LIMPING MAN

Right.

CLAIRE

I was seventeen.

LIMPING MAN

Uh-huh.

CLAIRE

And I came out of school and you were sitting in the front of your pick-up with a bunch of puppies on your lap.

KENNY

Mom, what are you doing?

CLAIRE

And you were tickling them and making faces. And you saw me and held one up and said, "Ain't this a cute one?" And we smiled at each other. And you reminded me of my father. And I thought, "I'm gonna marry that boy some day. Someone who is so much like my father must be so good inside."

LIMPING MAN

(pause)

That wathn't me, Claire.

CLAIRE

What?

LIMPING MAN

I never had no lap of puppeeth. I'm allergic.

CLAIRE

Allergic?

LIMPING MAN

And I never had a pick-up either. That wath your dad. That guy reminded you of your dad tho much becauthe it *wath* him. I'm allergic to puppeeth.

CLAIRE

Oh.

LIMPING MAN

Your couthin Jackie introduthed uth. At the Taco Bell?

CLAIRE

(not remembering)

Uh-huh.

LIMPING MAN

Claire . . .

CLAIRE

I . . . I . . . I'm not going with you.

LIMPING MAN

But Claire we just had that whole—

CLAIRE

I can't.

LIMPING MAN

Is it Kenny? Kenny can come too. I love Kenny.
(to KENNY)
You wanna come for a ride, kiddo?

CLAIRE

I feel awful about your ear and the limp and the lisp, and—

LIMPING MAN

The blindneth.

CLAIRE

Yeah, your blind eye, I feel bad about that too. But . . . maybe
I didn't have many choices.

LIMPING MAN

Thweetie . . .

CLAIRE

I don't know you. I don't think I ever did. And I don't have
any intention of taking up with strangers.

LIMPING MAN

But thath what you do every morning.

CLAIRE

I said no.

LIMPING MAN

(pause)
Okay. No ith no.
(beat)
I juth . . . worked tho hard on thith.
(moves in closer to her)
But I underthtand. And I'm thorry. You detherved better.

(He takes her hand affectionately. And after a beat
bends it back suddenly.)

LIMPING MAN

You ungrateful cunt!

(He's about to hit her, when KENNY *leaps on him and punches the wound on his back. The carnival music from the earlier scene blares in.)*

KENNY

Leave her alone! You piece of shit!

(They struggle for a couple beats, but PHILIP *is no match for* KENNY. KENNY *beats him into a corner.)*

LIMPING MAN

I'm thorry, honey! I thlipped!

CLAIRE

Stop it, Kenny! Please!

LIMPING MAN

It wath a lapthe. You made me upthet. Aren't I allowed thlipth?!

*(*KENNY's *rage is unrestrained. He kicks* PHIL, *throws things at him. The frozen food. Anything he can grab. He hurls it at* PHIL, *who's curled in a ball.)*

KENNY

After everything, you think you can come back and hit people?!

LIMPING MAN

I thwear I changed!

CLAIRE

Kenny! Don't do that!

LIMPING MAN

My thtitcheth are coming out!

KENNY

Good!
> *(hurls things at him)*

Good! Good! Good!

CLAIRE

Kenny! I said stop! You're like him! You're being like him!

> *(KENNY stops. He's out of breath and spent. The music is gone.)*

LIMPING MAN
> *(defeated, breathless)*

I'm good, Claire. I wath trying. I won't thlip again. Come with me.

> *(There's suddenly a huge crash and commotion from the basement and stairs.)*

HEIDI
> *(off)*

It's an ambush!

RICHARD
> *(off)*

Get back down here!

GERTIE
> *(off)*

Getta, Record!

HEIDI
> *(off)*

Help me, Phil!

> *(Then we hear the familiar sound of a shovel being thwacked across someone's head. HEIDI staggers in, rubbing her sore head. RICHARD follows her in, with a poised shovel. She collapses, out cold. RICHARD whips around and sees the defeated LIMPING MAN.)*

RICHARD

Hey . . . Hey! You got *him* and I got *her*! You twist his arm,
Kenny? Like I taught you?

KENNY

What?

RICHARD
       (referring to HEIDI*)*
Look at this one. I smashed her good and hard.
       (beat, then to CLAIRE*)*
Are you okay, honey?
       (beat)
Did I say something?

CLAIRE

Let's just call the police so I can go home.

       (GERTIE *runs into the kitchen with the puppet,
       pointing at it frantically.)*

GERTIE

Da doopy-guy ish baking pups!

MILLET
       (off)
Where's my Binky?!

CLAIRE

Aren't we done yet? I'm so tired.

       (MILLET *enters with hack saw.)*

MILLET

You gimme my puppet!

GERTIE
       (throws puppet at him)
Tay da fuddin puppa.

MILLET

(to CLAIRE*)*
And you gimme that ring!

CLAIRE

(gives him ring)
Here.

RICHARD

Hey, that's my ring.

MILLET

It's *not* your ring! It never was!
(as puppet)
I missed you, Millet.
(normal)
And I missed you, Binky.
(to everyone)
I'm taking my friend away from you people!
(puppet)
Liars and nutsos!
(normal)
We're gonna bring this ring back to the owner and clear my name. We'll start over!

LIMPING MAN

You can't, Millet.

MILLET

I'll tell them everything! And then they'll believe me! And I'll become a zoo keeper! You're bad people!
(puppet)
You're all crazy!
(runs out)

RICHARD

(pause)
There now. That wasn't so bad, was it? You're doing okay, Claire.

CLAIRE

Richard, don't tell me how I'm doing. Kenny, call the police. Gertie, you'll stay with us tonight.

GERTIE

Evatin kay nah, Clay. Evatin. Yukabe happy now. Happy-happy Clay.

(The lights fade on them. The sounds of cars transition us into—)

Scene Four

(Lights up in the car. KENNY and GERTIE are in the back seat. GERTIE's asleep. RICHARD drives. CLAIRE is beside him reading from her filo-fax book.)

RICHARD

Whataday-whataday-whataday.

CLAIRE

This book needs to be updated.

RICHARD

Aye-aye, General.

CLAIRE

There are a lot of things missing.

RICHARD

The doctors don't want you to know everything.

CLAIRE

Why not?

RICHARD

They said getting that upset every day would take its toll.

CLAIRE

On who?
        (beat)
Well, now that I'm fully informed and capable of making de-
cisions, I'm telling you to put it all in. The first sentence: Your
deformed husband beat you hard and often.

RICHARD

This is how you want to start your day?

CLAIRE

Just put it in.

RICHARD

You're the boss.

KENNY

Mom, you remember that blue sweater you made me?

CLAIRE

Sure, sweetie.

KENNY

It has a hole in it. You think you can fix it?

CLAIRE

We'll see.

RICHARD

Look at Gertie. All tuckered out. Been a long day for us, huh
Claire?

CLAIRE

How did we get married?

RICHARD

What?

CLAIRE

How did we get married?

RICHARD

Oh. Uhh . . . Well, you were in the hospital, and I saw you every day, and eventually I fell in love with you. Your sunny outlook. Your freshness.

KENNY

Your amnesia.

RICHARD

Not just that. Come on, Kenny . . .

CLAIRE

And what about *me*?

RICHARD

You?

CLAIRE

Did I agree to marry you?

RICHARD

Not the first eight times I asked. Once we made it as far as the license, and you backed out. But then one day I got lucky. You woke up in that hospital bed, and I was waiting with a cup of coffee and I said, "Good morning, Huckleberry" and you smiled at me. And I told you that I'd been in love with you for many months and we had shared a lot together and would you marry me. And you said okay. And the hospital chaplain came in, and all the paperwork was lined up from the last time, and he married us.

CLAIRE

(pause)
That's weird.

RICHARD

Weird?

CLAIRE

I didn't even know you.

RICHARD

Yes you did, sort of. I asked your mother. Kenny said it was okay.

KENNY

No I didn't. I said I didn't care.

RICHARD

Claire, I love you.

CLAIRE

No, I know. I mean . . . you seem nice enough. It's just— I don't know. I'm too tired to think straight.

RICHARD

Okay.

(*They drive on in silence.* CLAIRE *is close to falling asleep.*)

KENNY

Hey, Mom?

CLAIRE

Yeah?

KENNY

Don't go to sleep.

CLAIRE

It's been a long day.

KENNY

I know. I just want a couple more minutes.

CLAIRE

I'm sorry, honey. I'm fading.

RICHARD

Claire?

CLAIRE

Yeah?

RICHARD

What's my name?

CLAIRE

Richard Fiffle.

RICHARD

And who am I?

CLAIRE

(pause)
My husband.

RICHARD

Right. Good.
(beat)
You think tomorrow might be different?

CLAIRE

I don't know, Philip.

RICHARD

Richard.

CLAIRE

Right. Richard.
(beat)
Fix my book.

(CLAIRE *lies back and closes her eyes.*)

RICHARD

Maybe we won't need it. Maybe the alarm'll go off and you'll know me.

KENNY

Maybe you can drive me to school in the morning.

CLAIRE
(half-asleep)
Maybe.

RICHARD
Maybe our lives can go forward now. We can go for a walk in the park if you don't have anything planned.

KENNY
Or the movies.

RICHARD
Maybe tomorrow will be the second day of our marriage. And you'll say something like, "Remember that puppet that crazy guy had?" And I'll say, "Yeah."

KENNY
Maybe you'll remember everything. You think maybe, Mom?

RICHARD
Claire?

KENNY
Mom?

RICHARD
Claire?

KENNY
Mom?

(Silence. CLAIRE's asleep.

RICHARD and KENNY look at each other, then face the front. The lights slowly fade on them staring ahead as they drive into the darkness.)

Translation of Gertie's Stroke-Talk

A NOTE ON GERTIE'S SPEECH PATTERN: Strokes can affect people in countless ways. Language in particular can be dramatically impaired, often resulting in slurred speech or various forms of aphasia. Gertie's disorder is pretty straight-forward. Her words are simply jumbled. Syllables are often inverted, and similar-sounding words and sounds are substituted for the intended words. Gertie does not slur her words, talk slowly or have much difficulty speaking. The gibberish comes out effortlessly, without a struggle. Though she occasionally is very deliberate in her attempts to communicate, her speech patterns almost always have the same cadences and rhythms of someone who speaks normally. Gertie usually knows exactly what's she's trying to say in a very pointed way, while everyone around her is left to decipher the jumbled sentiments.

ACT ONE, SCENE THREE

Clay. Whadda dune hay? Youshen be gnome!
Claire, what are you doing here? You should be home.

Income, Clay. Income!
Come in, Claire. Come in!

Fee, whadda helen oodoo?
Philip, what the hell did you do?

Dashen dunder-mince-tate.
That's an understatement.

Fast break, Clay? Eggs? Sear-el? Toe-sat? Fast break?
Breakfast, Claire? Eggs? Cereal? Toast? Breakfast?

Balcony?
Bacon?

I jez hava fidful oh da balcony cuz yo foddeh lie dit so moo. I jez godden haboo oh keeboo da-roun oda tie.
I just have a fridge full of bacon because your father liked it so much. I just got into the habit of keeping some around all the time.

Ina la.
In the cellar.

I doan tink-toe, Clay.
I don't think so, Claire.

Clay, lessco fo wah, kay?

Claire, let's go for a walk, okay?

Isso ny ow sigh, lessco fo wah.

It's so nice outside, let's go for a walk.

Ya, da kenny. Buh Clay, lissa toe me, peas.

Yeah, the kennel. But Claire, listen to me, please.

No, Clay. Ida know no puppas!

No Claire. I don't know no puppets!

A basefreezer, Clay. Day basefreeze croquet.

A free-baser, Claire. They free-base cocaine.

Clay, noo-noo dish is gooey.

Claire, none of this is good.

Ees med ah noose bah.

These men are bad news.

Clay, dish is nah—

Claire, this is not—

Isis Geht Maso. Fee cape. Eesh ina hiss . . . Huh? . . . Fee cape . . .
***Cape* . . . Ee brogue adder summer . . . *Fee Cape!* . . . Geht Maso!**
. . . *Fee cape!!!*

This is Gertie Mason. Philip escaped. He's in the house . . . Huh? . . .
Philip escaped . . . *Escaped* . . . He broke out out of the slammer . . .
Philip escaped! . . . Gertie Mason! . . . *Philip escaped!!!*

Ish da rye? Dah isho fuddy.
Is that right? That is so funny.

Hoe-down do sicken.
Hold on a second.

Iyas mah frient . . . I cull mah frient . . . thall.
It was my friend . . . I called my friend . . . that's all.

No Fee, yoda ony baddy doo Clay.
No Philip, you've done only bad things to Claire.

ACT ONE, SCENE SEVEN

Trush noon by me, Clay.
Trust no one but me, Claire.

Dusha riddle dimsum da my hempoo.
Just a little something that might help you.

I doan tink toe!
I don't think so!

Dash ny!
That's nice!

Who do teching bat?
Who are you talking about?

Uh-huh. I bee rye bag.
Uh-huh. I'll be right back.

Pen-o, Clay. Toe-phoes.
Open, Claire. Photos.

Ada fay. Ih da fuhnus. Da meers.
At the fair. In the funhouse. The mirrors.

Ih da fuhnus. Fuddy meers.
In the funhouse. Funny mirrors.

In Piehmoe.
In Piermont.

Da Piehmoe fay!
The Piermont Fair!

An da Za in da fuddy meers.
And that's Zack in the funny mirrors.

Yada tooda pitue oh Za ih da fuddy meers.
Your Dad took the picture of Zack in the funny mirrors.

Edadly!
Exactly!

Da ih Za, Clay. He feh oh da tee.
That is Zack, Claire. He fell out of the tree.

You doe mem ohta tins dah happy.
You don't remember all the things that happened.

Yesh! Da fyin' pay!
Yes! The frying pan!

Dogdambit!
Goddamit!

Cursive. Ida nevoo crotch you.
Of course. I'd never cross you.

Noda Za, Clay. Ee feh oh da tee.
That's not Zack, Claire. He fell out of the tree.

Yuca keelush, Fee, buhda woe cha-cha nuddy!
You can kill us, Philip, but it won't change nothing!

Ree, Clay! Ree!
Read, Claire! Read!

Ih tess wha happy!
It tells what happened!

Egg dis!
Take this!

Isis Geht Maso. _Fee Cape_! . . . I dabbed him inda bag!
This is Gertie Mason. _Philip Escaped_! . . . I stabbed him in the back!

Ona four ohda clickin! Oh, dear heah!
On the floor of the kitchen! Oh, they're here!

No! Iss my pho! Fug dew!
No! This is my phone! Fuck you!

Ah! My pho!
Ah! My phone!

Dab da fuddin puppa!
Stab the fuckin' puppet!

Kee da puppa! Doopy fuddin' puppa! Die! Die!
Kill the puppet! Stupid fuckin' puppet! Die! Die!

ACT TWO, SCENE ONE

An noon onion stammy!
And no one understands me!

Ish axel is genderlish!
This asshole is dangerous!

Ee hersh poopoos!
He hurts people!

I doan onion stammish.
I don't understand this.

Ida gnome mower, Clay. Evatin' row when Za feh oda tee. Da die. Oomay Fee an bah tin happy. Deh oo fie bah an deh figit. An I hada toke, so king talk bah. Fee heah an evatin' bah gin. Evatin' bah gin, Clay.
I don't know anymore, Claire. Everything went wrong when Zack fell out of the tree. Dad died. You married Philip and bad things happened. Then you fight back and then forget. And I had a stroke, so I'm talking bad. Philip's here and everything's bad again. Everything's bad again, Claire.

ACT TWO, SCENE TWO

Dash biggo yoo-zo doopy.
That's because you're so stupid.

Yah. Maybe ova nose bachus.
Yeah. Maybe over in those boxes.

Uh . . . Oday. Aybee ride bag.
Uh . . . Okay. I'll be right back.

Nuddin' fuddy heah.
Nothing funny here.

Ahm dill loodin'!
I'm still looking!

I tink iss up in da clickin.
I think it's up in the kitchen.

I gut da doe-in-tit.
I've got the sewing kit.

Loo ah dese toe-phos, Record.
Look at these photos, Richard.
Loo ah dis one dough. Is da weddin' dah.
Look at this one though. It's the wedding day.

Sumna-bitch.
Sonofabitch.

I coo tah den. Bach den evabiddy onion stammy. I wizz-eye hat . . . Iiii wiissh . . . I had . . . sehd sssummttiiinnn weeeehnn . . . I c-could.

I could talk then. Back then everybody understood me. I wish I had . . . I wish . . . I had . . . said . . . something when . . . I could.

Digga widda shova.

Digging with the shovel.

Aybee rye bag.

I'll be right back.

Toe-phoes! Thall! Toe-phoes!

Photos! That's all! Photos!

Dem pick gog shit! Fuddin' shit!

Damn prick goddam shit! Fucking shit!

I'm loodin'!

I'm looking!

I ding I fow da bach, Record!

I think I found the box, Richard!

Damma fuddin' shova!

Damn this fucking shovel!

I guddit!

I've got it!

ACT TWO, SCENE THREE

Heddo, dis geddin da doe-in-tit.

Hello, just getting the sewing kit.

I gut da doe-in-tit.

I've got the sewing kit.

Getta, Record!

Get her, Richard!

Da doopy-guy ish baking pups!

The stupid guy is waking up!

Tay da fuddin' puppa.

Take the fuckin' puppet.

Evatin' kay nah, Clay. Evatin'. Yukabe happy nah. Happy, happy Clay.

Everything's okay now, Claire. Everything. You can be happy now. Happy, happy Claire.